LUZ ARGENTINA CHIRIBOGA

On Friday Night

Translated by

Paulette A. Ramsay

and

Anne-María Bankay

A r a w a k publications
17 Kensington Crescent
Kingston 5 Jamaica

 Published 2009

ISBN 978 976 8189 73 8

12 11 10 9
d c b a

UWI LIBRARY CATALOGUING IN PUBLICATION DATA

Luz Argentina Chiriboga
En la noche del viernes. English
On Friday night / by Luz Argentina Chiriboga ; translated by
Paulette A. Ramsay and Anne-María Bankay

p. cm.
ISBN 978-976-8189-73-8

I. Ramsay, Paulette A. II. Bankay, Anne-María
III. Title 1: En la noche del viernes IV. Title 2: On Friday night.

PQ7409.2.C62 E513 2009 868.992

Cover design by Errol Stennett
Book design by Annika Lewinson-Morgan

Set in 10/14pt Schniedler BT with Amaryllis and Amaryllis Swash DB

Contents

Acknowledgments

Thanks to the author, Luz Argentina Chiriboga, for providing the opportunity to translate her work and for being available for consultation on different matters.

Errol Stennett for his beautiful cover artwork.

Althea Aiken for typing.

Professors Keith Ellis and Patrick Bryan for reading the manuscript and for their helpful suggestions.

Karen Henry for proofreading and advice on translation.

Monica Parris, Julette Lawson, Ouida Lodge-Jones and Stephany Blair for their reassuring strength.

Our families for their encouragement and support.

Introduction

LUZ ARGENTINA CHIRIBOGA (1940–)

This Afro-Ecuadorian writer was born in 1940 in Esmeraldas, the Ecuadorian province which is predominantly inhabited by descendants of black slaves. She undertook formal studies in Biology at the Universidad Central in Quito, Ecuador where she currently resides. Chiriboga is well known for her research and publications on Ecuador's African derived heritage, for her role as defender of the rights of African descendants in Ecuador, and for her involvement in the women's movement in her country where she has served as president of the National Union of Ecuadorian Women.

Chiriboga was married to the distinguished Afro-Ecuadorian writer Nelson Estupiñán Bass, with whom she shared the passion for literature and an interest in Afro-Latin American culture in general and Ecuadorian African derived heritage in particular. Before her husband's death in 2003, they travelled extensively together to participate in several international conferences on Afro-Latin American culture and delivered numerous lectures in the United States on Ecuadorian literature and culture. Currently, she continues her research on Ecuadorian history and Afro-Ecuadorian oral tradition – subjects which hold great intellectual and cultural importance for her.

Chiriboga's works have been included in anthologies published both nationally and internationally. In 1986 she was awarded the General José de San Martín prize in Buenos Aires, Argentina. She continues to be an active member of various literary and cultural societies and organizations, among them, the Sociedad de Amigos de la Genealogía, Grupo América, Sociedad Ecuatoriana de Escritores, and the Club Social Cultural de Esmeraldas.

Luz Argentina Chiriboga is regarded as one of Ecuador's most prolific and important writers. Her creative works include fiction as well as poetry. Her narratives include – *Bajo la piel de los tambores / Drums Under My Skin* (1991), *Jonatás y Manuela* (1994) and *En la noche del viernes / On Friday Night* (1999). Her collections of poetry include *La contaportada del deseo / The Back Cover of Desire* (1992), *Palenque: décimas* (1999) and *Coplas esmeraldeñas / Esmeraldan Coplas* (2000). She has also published other non-literary works based on her research into Ecuadorian culture and history. These include *Diáspora: por los caminos de Esmeraldas / (Diaspora: Through the Roads of Esmeraldas)* (1997), *Luis Vargas Torres y los niños / (Luis Vargas Torres and the Children)* (2001), *Manual de ecología / Manual of Ecology* (1992), and *Escritores esmeraldeños / Esmeraldan Writers* (1995).

When *Bajo la piel de los tambores / Drums Under My Skin* was translated by Mary Harris in 1996, it became the first Ecuadorian novel to be translated to English. The first part of *Jonatás y Manuela* was translated by Rosemary Geisdorfer Feal and several of her poems have also been translated by different scholars and included in a range of significant collections, such as *Daughters of the Diaspora* (2003).

Chiriboga's creative works focus on bringing Afro-Ecuadorian culture centre stage, rewriting the history of Afro-Ecuadorians, underlining their contribution to the development of Ecuadorian society and asserting black female subjectivity and agency. Chiriboga, who claims that she is conscious of her responsibility as a writer in a society which has inherited principles based on slavery and oppression, asserts:

> The education system in Ecuador excludes the values of Afro-Ecuadorian culture; the result is that others do not know our contribution to the society. One of my functions, therefore, is to raise the self-esteem of Afro-Ecuadorians and promote pride in our African ancestry, reaffirm identity and reject their feelings of inferiority resulting from the years of cultural oppression to which they have been subjected (Chiriboga 64).

CHIRIBOGA'S POETRY

Chiriboga characterizes poetry as "un espacio abierto a la verdad"/ "a space open to truth" (Chiriboga 65). In keeping with this view of the genre, she has produced poems which belong to a range of categories – social, erotic, ecological, historical and children's poetry – and in them, she explores a wide gamut of themes.

La contraportada del deseo / The Back Cover of Desire (1992) comprises some of her most erotic writings, as she celebrates the black woman's subjectivity and confidence in her identity as a black woman. Chiriboga writes explicitly about the black woman's sexuality, employing very erotic images. It is a collection which could be regarded as reinforcing some traditional stereotypes about the black woman as a naturally and primarily sensuous being, given its overt focus on her physical beauty and sexual appeal. Simultaneously however, it defies these stereotypes in the celebration of Afro-centric beauty as an ideal way of being rather than as an allurement or sexual enticement. Moreover, the black woman is presented as one of many attributes, who is strong and in full control of her life and sexuality.

In *Palenque: décimas* (1999), her second collection of poetry, Luz Argentina focuses on and celebrates a wide range of subjects, but particularly the affirmation of the struggle for liberation by different generations of people of African descent in Latin America. The title *Palenque: décimas* functions as the ideological frame of reference for the work as the author celebrates the resilience, achievements and distinctions gained by the descendants of slaves in various parts of the black diaspora (Ramsay 116).

The poems have been composed as *décimas* which are taken from the oral tradition of the Afro-Ecuadorian people of Esmeraldas. Chiriboga's use of the *décima* is sophisticated and shows her ability to use assonance and rhyme in an effective and gripping manner. Through the various thematic impulses, Chiriboga creates her own metaphorical *palenque* – her work of poetic refuge in which she is free to meditate on and vindicate her heritage of resistance and her African derived oral tradition (Ramsay 119).

Luis Vargas Torres y los niños / Luis Vargas Torres and the Children (2001) is a collection of poems written in honour of Colonel Luis Vargas Torres, an Esmeraldan who led the 1883 war against the dictatorship of Ignacio de Veintemilla, ending years of military tyranny in Ecuador. Luis Vargas is celebrated in Esmeraldas as a great martyr, hero and son of the region. Chiriboga composed the poems on behalf of the people of Esmeraldas in commemoration of his 114th birthday and to celebrate his work, philosophy and political ideology.

Coplas esmeraldeñas / Esmeraldan Coplas (2001) is a compilation of Afro-Esmeraldan *coplas*, a popular lyrical composition or ballad which varies in length from three to five lines of eight to twelve syllables each. Chiriboga's *coplas* were compiled over a number of years during which she traversed the province of Esmeraldas collecting these verses, which are being threatened into extinction by the influence of radio, television and other modes of communication. The *coplas* convey several themes – some extol the virtues which make a person honourable, some present both males and females, highlighting each others' flaws, but the most crucial contribution of the *coplas* is their affirmation of the African oral tradition which has been preserved by Afro-Ecuadorians.

CHIRIBOGA'S NOVELS

The novel, for Chiriboga, is the form which facilitates greatest fluidity between genres, as it holds possibilities for the incorporation of other genres such as poetry, drama, documents and newspaper articles (Chiriboga 65). The black woman is the central focus of Chiriboga's fictive world. From her first novel, *Bajo la piel de los tambores* (1991), considered to be the first black female authored prose fiction in Afro-Hispanic and Latin American literatures, she confronts the problem of discrimination on the basis of race and class. Consequently, she has created a discourse that addresses issues affecting black women, which had hitherto been ignored by male-authored texts, in which black female characters are either invisible or are presented in marginal and mainly subservient roles.

Bajo la piel de los tambores dismantles traditional constructions of race, class and gender in Hispanic society. Through Rebecca, the black female protagonist, the author explores the uncertainties, contradictions and ambiguities that are often displayed by black women in societies in which racial heritage, social and economic background impinge on the formation of one's identity. Through Rebecca's struggles with her conflicts about her sexuality, her identity, her heritage and her determination to discover herself, the author subverts traditional notions of black female sexuality, and disrupts conventional concepts of social norms. Rebecca moves from self-doubting and denial of her people and class to attain an education which enables her to understand the social and racial inequities of her society and to attempt to establish a sense of autonomy and an independent identity, as a black woman in a white dominated racist society.

Chiriboga's preoccupation with history is evident in her second novel *Jonatás y Manuela* in which she fictionalizes the history of enslavement of Ba-Lunda, an African woman, and her black slave, Manuela Sáenz. Manuela participates in several slave revolts and armed struggles for Ecuador's emancipation and independence. Through her fictional representation of historical accounts, Chiriboga underlines the contribution of the black slave woman to the struggles for liberation and independence in Latin America, thereby, giving attention to another aspect of Ecuadorian history which had previously been muted.

ON FRIDAY NIGHT

On Friday Night is a novel which unfolds in two narrative strands. The more extensive and dominant strand develops the narrative of a young girl who receives a bouquet of flowers on her doorstep every Friday night, from a mysterious admirer, who is eventually revealed to be Marvin Mann, her white neighbour and the father of her childhood playmates, Margarita and Jaime. A complex story of passion, disillusionment, racism and betrayal unfolds, as Susana seeks to understand herself, her feelings and to establish subjectivity and agency in a complex society.

Susana develops an awareness of the social realities involving race and class in her society at an early age, as she is conscienticized by a strong, black-conscious grandmother, who helps her to develop an understanding of herself as a black woman in a racist society. But when Susana is devastated by the deception of Ruperto, her first boyfriend, and her best friend Luz Argentina, she ignores the reservations expressed by her grandmother and yields to the offers of comfort from Marvin Mann, eventually marrying him.

At first, Susana struggles with fears and uncertainties about being attracted to a much older man and one of a different racial and social background which is perceived by society to be superior to her own background and race. However, their marriage becomes an act of defiance on the part of both characters, against a society which classifies people according to race and class and dictates all their activities, including their romantic interests. The differences between Susana and Marvin are pronounced, and are dramatized by various details of their lives – their age, preferences in music, levels of maturity, overall approach to life and, of course, their racial and social background and the associations society makes with these. Susana reveals her awareness of these differences and how they inform the specious views of some in the society in one of her narrated monologues:

> Marvin did everything calmly, too slowly, with too much discipline. All of that was very different for me as I did everything quickly, everything was changing.
> Unconsciously he clung to order and unconsciously I clung

> to disorder, to breaking rules. He spoke calmly, pronouncing his words carefully whereas I used gestures to replace words. He danced the *tango*, I the *merengue*. He wanted to become part of my world. He was aware of my youth; he didn't want anything to separate us. He wanted to prolong my joy, my freshness. He was tolerant of my pranks because he thought that losing me would be to lose himself. He gave thanks to God that his desires had been granted and on the honeymoon we went to the beach to daydream and pretended not to hear: 'Look, a black girl with a white man. What a stupid white man' (104).

The title of the work *On Friday Night* draws attention to the ambiguities and contradictions of Susana's relationship with Marvin. She comes to associate Friday nights with the beautiful bouquets/illusions from the admirer, but Friday night is also the night her grandmother leaves mysteriously, after perceiving in her own clairvoyant way, that the bouquet which on the surface seems to hold the prospect of happiness for Susana will also bring great unhappiness for her:

> She left one Friday when on opening the door to the hallway she found a bouquet of dreams, the day that she sensed that a wealthy white man with a calm, kind, relaxed love, loved her granddaughter but that her granddaughter deserved much more. "It's a mistake," she said. Nobody knew what she was talking about. That day she went away because she did not want to be witness to the path that Susana's life would take, a path from which it would be impossible to escape (17).

The insidious tension created by their marriage is exacerbated by the attitude of Marvin's daughter Margarita, who capitalizes on every opportunity to undermine and destroy the relationship. Eventually, the relationship itself is exposed to be destined for disaster as Marvin himself is not unlike the much younger

Susana, unsure of himself and the security of his marriage to a young, beautiful, desirable black woman. When one of his daughter's schemes to create suspicions about Susana's fidelity succeeds, Marvin reveals in what becomes a painful discovery for Susana, the extent to which he himself has imbibed the racist principles of his society. In his anger, Marvin reveals his deep-seated attitude toward blacks and the extent to which he has made an exception, for numerous reasons, to be in this relationship with Susana:

> You Negroes have deep hatred. From everywhere ghosts come pursuing you, making you contemptible. You are ungrateful. Margarita took you to the bank (106).

Susana discovers the painful truth that while he desires her sexually, his entire psycho-system has been so shaped by the racist ideologies of his society that he still rejects her as a social equal. Her awakening to this subtle link between racial discrimination and sexual exploitation is painful. On discovering the duplicity in Marvin's attitude, Susana retreats into self-doubting and silence and finds solace only in her *guitarra* and her grandmother's stories, feeling strongly that she has betrayed everything that is important to her as a black woman:

> He intruded into my intimate world, into what runs through my veins and genes. I would have given everything I had to retrace my steps if it were possible... I noticed that something was burning inside me, what was most sacred to me: my parents, my grandmother, my ancestry, my history (106).

In the end, Susana, who is no longer able to endure Marvin's unpredictability and her alienation from her peers, succumbs to the attention being shown to her by

Marvin's son, Jaime, with whom she had played and swum naked in her childhood years. The apocalyptic ending of the novel highlights the complexity, ambiguities and uncertainties of Susana's existence. We are left with an image of her as one who has not really successfully achieved agency, as her husband Marvin stands above her and Jaime in passionate embrace, his gun aimed at them, showing that he is still in control of her and is unwilling to allow her to make choices of her own for her own future happiness.

On an initial reading, the minor narrative strand seems to be totally distinct and unrelated to the major one with characters and images which are totally disconnected. Closer examination of these strands however, reveals that there are balanced interactions between the two. The major strand involving the central character Susana repeatedly presents situations which contrast with the secondary strand with Moconga, the female character who emigrates to the United States and becomes famous for her achievements. In fact, in the initial stages of the novel, there is a brief encounter between Susana's father and Moconga's father, but this link is not sustained. While Susana is searching for meaning in her life, Moconga is confidently charting the course of her life. Susana's frustrations and periods of unhappiness contrast with Moconga's happiness and self-assurance. Susana's plight at the end of the work is made more poignant by Moconga's success.

Moconga is therefore the antithesis of Susana, being more self-assured and committed to her African cultural heritage which becomes the ideological frame within which she structures her life. Moconga symbolizes love, solidarity and the embracing of blackness/negritude.

She is also the vanguard of feminism in the work as at an early age she exhibits a determination to exert personal agency and desire to take control of the direction of her life. Through Moconga, the writer creates a model of a black woman who chooses to affirm aspects of her culture and take pragmatic steps to develop a spirit of *camaraderie* with fellow blacks. The lasting image of Moconga is one of an independent, self-certain young woman, unlike that of Susana, who simply spins a web of confusion around herself.

Luz Argentina Chiriboga is fully aware of the racial and social context in which she produces her creative works. Moreover, she completely accepts the dual responsibility of being a black female writer in a country which she characterizes as one in which "discrimination on the basis of race and class is profound... even though it is not discussed" (Chiriboga 64). This knowledge of the racial and social stereotypes about blacks greatly influences the portrayal of the black grandmother in *On Friday Night* (1999). This is a black woman who, conscious of her own marginalization and the exclusion of her African derived cultural heritage from the mainstream of society, performs various acts of resistance against the stereotyping of both her race and class. She is involved in a determined struggle to preserve her cultural heritage, redefine her identity and defy cultural domination.

Chiriboga uses the character of Matilde to respond to the notion of her people as being without culture or having an inferior culture. Hence, Matilde opposes the manner in which her descendants have accepted and assimilated new cultural practices. She therefore assumes responsibility for educating her family about the values of their own cultural tradition as part of her insistence on preserving a unique identity for herself and her family – an identity that is distinct from the categories in which they have been placed and which some have accepted. Matilde does not only accept the role as custodian of the traditions of the family but has also defined and practised the same values which she wants to impart to her granddaughter Susana. Indeed, we are given a picture of how Matilde maintains a constant presence in Susana's life from the time of her birth, ensuring that she receives adequate education at each stage of her development, and inculcates in Susana solid spiritual values to help her develop her own spirituality within an Afro-centric frame of reference.

Through the many stories which Matilde narrates to Susana, she transmits collective values which are central to Susana's development of a consciousness of her ancestral roots and their relation to a collective history of mental and physical control. In her time of crisis when she is most painfully and directly confronted by the harsh realities of racism, Susana recalls her grandmother's project to help her to preserve herself. When Susana eventually recognizes the need to reinvent herself in order to survive the harsh realities of her marriage, she has already departed from her grandmother's teachings.

In the novel's denouement, her grandmother's fears that she has chosen a path of destruction become reality. Susana, while being an interesting, self-motivating young woman, is simultaneously an ambiguous character. She is fascinated by and carries her cultural heritage deep in her psycho-system, but she is not defined by it.

Paulette A. Ramsay
2006

Notes

[1] Norman E. Whitten Jr., Diego Quiroga and P. Rafael Savoia, "Ecuador," in *No Longer Invisible: Afro-Latin Americans Today*, ed. Pedro Pérez-Sarduy & Jean Stubbs (London: Minority Rights Group Publications, 1995), 291.

References

Chiriboga, Luz Argentina. *Bajo la piel de los tambores*. Quito, Ecuador: Editorial Casa de la Cultura Ecuatoriana, 1991.

———. *Manual de ecología*. Quito: Abrapalabra Editores, 1992.

———. *La contraportada del deseo*. Quito: Abya Ayala, 1992.

———. *Jonatás y Manuela*. Quito: Abrapalabra Editores, 1994.

———. *Escritores esmeraldeños: raíces, biografía, producción, y crítica*. Tomos 1,2,3. Quito: Editorial e Imprenta Delta, 1995.

———. *Diáspora por los caminos de Esmeraldas*. Quito: Ardilla Editores, 1997.

———. *Tambores bajo mi piel: novela*. Tercera edición. Quito: Editorial Instituto andino de artes populares (IADAP), 1999.

———. *Palenque: décimas*. Quito: Editorial IADAP, 1999.

———. *Luis Vargas Torres y los niños*. Quito: Ediciones Consejo Provincial de Esmeraldas , 2001.

Geisdorfer Feal, Rosemary. "The Legacy of Ba-Lunda: Black Female Subjectivity in Luz Argentina Chiriboga's *Jonatás y Manuela*". *Afro-Hispanic Review* 17, no. 2 (1998).

———. "The Poetics and Politics of Desire: Eroticism in Luz Argentina Chiriboga's *Bajo la piel de los tambores*." In *Daughters of the Diaspora*, ed. Miriam DeCosta Willis, 213-24. Kingston, Jamaica: Ian Randle Publishers, 2003.

Seales Soley, La Verne M., and Sharon P. Seales Soley. "Entrevista con Luz Argentina Chiriboga: escritora afro-ecuatoriana". *Afro-Hispanic Review* 17, no. 3 (1998): 64-66.

Ramsay, Paulette A. Review Article. *Palenque: décimas*. *PALARA*, no. 4 (fall 2000): 116-20.

———. Review Article. *Coplas esmeraldeñas*. *PALARA*, no. 7 (2003): 89-91.

Whitten, Norman Jr., Diego Quiroga, and P. Rafael Savoia. "Ecuador." In *No Longer Invisible: Afro-Latin Americans Today*, ed. Pedro Pérez-Sarduy & Jean Stubbs. London: Minority Rights Group Publications, 1995.

On Translating

EN LA NOCHE DEL VIERNES

The story line of *En la noche del viernes* centers on the love that develops between an older man from the upper stratum of Ecuadorian society and a young girl from a much lower economic level. Their relationship provides the author with a legitimate reason to explore the social issues – race, class, exploitation, injustice, prejudice, to name a few – which existed in Ecuador during the height of cocoa production.

These social issues, more than anything else, need to be communicated in translating this work. As such, meaning and content were primary concerns in creating an English version of Luz Argentina Chiriboga's work. Fidelity was therefore an important consideration in the translation of this work. Although the translator of a literary piece is concerned with preserving, as fully as possible, a certain genre or style, his/her responsibility with regard to the finished product requires that a delicate balance between the "intention of the author, the target language and the target audience" be maintained, as indicated by Albir (1990: 118) in her study of fidelity in translation. Nevertheless, the translators were sometimes faced with the reality of tipping the balance in favour of communicating the author's message to the detriment of slavishly preserving her style.

Because, too, the style of Chiriboga's writing in this text is quite complex – truncated sentences, abrupt switches from one subject pronoun to another, invented or altered words to maintain a rhythm – it would have been difficult, sometimes even impossible, to maintain and reproduce this style of writing in English. For example, English does not have the range of gender specific pronouns, nor does it have the variety of ways to express 'you', depending on the nature of the speaker's relationship with the person(s) addressed. There was no attempt, in the Glissant sense (1958), to transform the work, to 'create' an almost entirely new entity.

Another consideration in translating this text relates to the ideology of the writer. This subtly permeates accounts of the social situations which she describes. The translators remained true to the ideological position adopted by the author and no attempt was made to excise this ideology from the translated version or to 'sterilize' it in any way.

When translating, knowledge of both languages may not, in and of itself, be sufficient. To capture the essence, the ambience, of the period about which the author writes, it is necessary to get information, details, outside of the published work. This is what is referred to by Durieux (1995: 20) as "thematic knowledge, that indispensable background to the area from which the writing is drawn". In this case, the translator's general and thematic knowledge assists in providing a 'feel' for the period, making it possible to select the appropriate words and expressions that are consistent with the way people express themselves, or even to gain insights into their thought processes and perspectives, if the time period is a factor. The translator's role as researcher, one of his/her basic skills, becomes very important in this context. The required information may be obtained from historical accounts of the period and even from other texts, whether literary or pragmatic.

As with many translations, in particular those in the

literary genre, there are words in the source language which have no exact equivalent in the target language. The best that can be done is a paraphrase or an explanatory translation in an effort to convey the meaning. On the other hand, some words are kept in the source language so as to maintain some 'feel' for the culture of the country and its language. Also, in literary translations the translator faces a challenge when the form of the source text is poetic, as is the case with songs and poetry. Very often, puns and subtle shades of meaning abound and require skillful handling by the translator. In this text, for example, there is a poem which plays on the two meanings of the Spanish word 'pluma' – feather and pen. Happily, 'quill' in English was a suitable equivalent, and though somewhat archaic, it was still appropriate for the time period. In this instance, the search for an equivalent meant that due attention had to be paid to the historical context of the source text without disregard for the overall effect of the new text on the new audience. In other words, the word 'quill' satisfied the exigencies of faithfulness to the 'letter' by being the best corresponding word, as well as faithfulness to the 'spirit' of the translation by being the best equivalence in meaning (Ladmiral 1979).

Two translators worked on *En la noche....* Two persons or more working together have the advantage of being able to consult each other so as to clarify doubts, as well as to get another 'interested and informed' opinion on subtleties of meaning, for example. This is extremely important if the goal is to produce a translation of a very high quality. Additionally, for this work it was possible to speak with the author herself, who provided explanations as to her choice of expression or her intentions when the meaning was cloudy. Had this not been so, some aspects of the text could have been lost in translation.

Anne-María Bankay
2007

References

Durieux, Christine. *Apprendre à traduire*. Paris: La Maison du Dictionnaire, 1995.
Glissant, Edouard. *La Lézarde*. Paris: Editions du Seuil, 1958.
Hurtado-Albir, A. *La notion de fidélité en traduction*. Paris: Didier Erudition, 1990.
Ladmiral, J.-R. *Théorèmes pour la traduction*. Paris: Payot, 1979.

LUZ ARGENTINA CHIRIBOGA

On Friday Night

Everything is movement, everything undulates: the wind, the clouds, the river, the palms, the water in the tank, the birds. I sing the latest *merengue*. I slide my feet from side to side and I smile, thankful for life. I remember Saturdays in the home of the Mann family; they seemed like a *fiesta*. We would savour *turrones* with almond fillings that Margarita's and Jaime's grandmother sent for her relatives.

"Eat, Susana," Marvin would say.

I had seen them inside a crystal candy box which they had in the centre of the dining table. Afterwards we would run out to the yard and play basketball. When the ball went into the hoop, Mr. Mann applauded. We played statue: we didn't breathe so as not to move; whoever lost had to go and kiss the mad woman in the area. In the winter season we would take off our clothes so they would not get dirty. Sweat made our skin sticky. We would put on our short pants and go to wade in the puddles formed by the rain. In the Mann's yard, there were palm trees which we climbed without shoes. At first we couldn't climb them but after some months we managed to reach the top, and we would sit and look at the river which from that height looked like a silver ribbon. I remember also that when it was Saturday in the summer, we built a fire, cooked plantains, eggs and a chicken which we stole from the neighbour's house, and ate inside a hut made from palm leaves.

The Manns always lived in the same house. All their things shone; they were colourful and the air one breathed there smelt of flowers. When I got to my house, I would run and bathe with the water from the tank as my legs would be covered with mud. I always used to hear that the city would soon have drinking water. The inhabitants had worms and pale faces, which is why in our house we always boiled the water. Flies took advantage of the ponds to breed in them. At the end of winter an anti-malaria campaign team fumigated the yards and houses with DDT. I remember that my parents used to throw soil on the mudhole which the rain formed and they would sweep the yard so that we could play hopscotch. Mama did not give up the things of the countryside and so she used to rear a rooster. She was accustomed to him waking her up at dawn.

I remember also listening to Marvin: Ruth, understand this, we must love children. Allow Susana to play with our children; she is a harmless child. I asked her what she wants to be when she grows up and she said a lawyer. Ruth, why does that make you laugh¿ What you must do is offer her soursop ice-cream. You have the magic formula; it is delicious. No Ruth, you are wrong, she doesn't stop being a little child simply because she's black. Eventually Ruth began to get accustomed to my presence.

So many years living near the Mann family, how could I not think about it¿ Jaime with a leg resting on my body; Jaime soaping up my back in the rain and I feeling ticklish; Jaime inside the hut and I at his side feeling his wet skin.

When Marvin caressed his children he would embrace me; I would feel his smell clinging to my body and all of him seemed to linger with me. His heart would beat faster and he and I would smile without knowing the reason for our happiness. I saw him like papa who had everything for me to love him.

When Susana's body seemed drained by the summer heat she no longer went to the Mann's house but continued to reminisce about that marvellous reality. It was the focus of her thoughts. It was like laughing and crying at the same time. Susana made a pact with herself to control her feelings and she decided to forget forever the idea of being in love with the Manns. She analysed the situation, put her thoughts in order and devoted her attention to her studies for her high school diploma. After two months she received her diploma and she hung it in her bedroom. Carlota was happy since her daughter was now someone. For the graduation party, Susana and Luz Argentina dressed in identical suits which looked like pale pink dresses with low necklines which showed the navel. La Garcés borrowed wigs from a beauty salon and Manolo did the make-up. And so, they arrived at the party where many persons asked who had invited such important persons since they said they were Sofía and María, the famous actress and her sister. It was only when the programme announced La Garcés' participation in the interpretation of two musical pieces that they realized who that woman with provocative lips and body like a palm tree was. At that moment she did not know if the applause was for the best disguise or for the music which Susana's fingers plucked from the *guitarra*. Afterwards they proposed a toast to each other's success, for the loves they would have; and they even cried at the pain of separation – some of them had been friends since the first grade of school.

Several schoolmates took photographs embracing each other. There was no shortage of those who embraced more than necessary because of nostalgia. When the drinks were finished they asked Susana to continue playing the *guitarra*. She accepted the request and played for that man who sent her best wishes and cried even though she didn't know him. It was the first time that La Garcés and her neighbour Luz Argentina did not sleep at home. They arrived with wigs in hand, *guitarra* on the shoulder, eyes swollen from crying and not knowing where they were. On opening the door of the hallway, Carlota smelled alcohol and faced the new high school graduate but Susana threw herself in her bed with clothes, make-up and her *guitarra*, and in between dreams she heard her mother who continued scolding her, "You'll have to buy your liquor with the sweat of your brow."

Besides the challenge of her mother, at the moment she had the feeling of being in a body that was not hers. Her mind wandered in directions she had never taken before. What disturbed her most was the feeling of being watched by two blue eyes. She covered her face with the pillow but in spite of that, the stares continued. She went stumbling to the bathroom and pushed two fingers down her throat to vomit. She looked at herself in the mirror and on seeing her face next to Marvin's she fainted. When she regained consciousness, she cried. It is not possible to love that old man, she said pounding the floor. Then she curled up in a corner like a wounded animal.

The wind still fluttered the sheets which were hanging on the lines and created noises like those of the beetle. At that time the sun had set and the shadows of the palm trees were getting longer. I loved the coastline at that time because that was when it got cooler. The city wore a flimsy dress and the hustle and bustle decreased. The shouting, singing, calls to buy mangoes, cow's milk, cheese, avocado for the honeymoon all stopped. Everything that was one big hubbub deserted the waterfront.

Soon there would be strangers sitting on the porches on boxes which would serve as mats, savouring the smells of the river and the colours painted by the moon on the islets. They would enjoy the voice of Julio Jaramillo floating on the air between the heaps of charcoal and garbage from the jukeboxes located in the gully. They would entertain themselves by repeating poems they had learnt during childhood, while the motel owners prepared food for nocturnal passers-by. They seemed to be getting ready to find God among the first lights of the stars. Newly arrived peasants would caress the machetes which they carried in their waist and exchange signals as greetings. Children walked barefooted in search of some fallen fruit and laughed heartily when they found some, happy to know that with it they could satisfy their hunger somewhat. Around the corner was the mad woman who talked about the same topic to herself every day: "That son of a bitch sold my house and went away with another woman." She wore a torn up blouse which had been tied into a knot to hide her bosom. She walked slowly, stumbling; she was pregnant. Mama would send food to her in a plastic plate and after eating she would lie down on the porch and smile as if she were giving God thanks.

My community was always filled with noises from vehicles which never switched off their engines, wheelbarrows, loaders, passengers, prostitutes, marijuana smokers, religious persons who proclaimed divine salvation. There, day after day, people would sing a love song to my sadness. My community, which became a fish market, flower shop, liquor store, watch maker's, shoe store, tobacco shop, drug store, banana stall, fruit market and charcoal shop, opened its arms every day to offer warm refuge to the poor.

One afternoon Luz Argentina came as usual to share gossip, our way of extending our affection to others. She usually wore lycra and short T-shirts. Sometimes she chose stretch jeans. When it was warm she would wear shorts and a long blouse. We were flamboyant in our affection for each other. She was more robust than I, her buttocks were more pronounced than mine. She was my friend, my confidante, she became the sister my parents hadn't given me. I began to think of her as a being that was out of this world; I attributed extraordinary qualities to her. We laughed about our graduation photographs and then she laughed because a car that was passing splashed mud all over Manolo's shirt. She laughed because the oldest man in the city died and she laughed because a client at the boutique where she worked gave her a bad cheque; she was a cascade of laughter and happiness.

When mama's hands hurt her, she would come with grapes: "Carlota my dear, open your mouth and eat a grape, one for your dear husband, one for your daughter and one for your friend." Mama would laugh at her wittiness. She would walk with her arms spread like the wings of birds that wanted to fly to other places. We would talk until the light of the sky paled behind our backs. She moved her eyes like a squirrel, but on other occasions silence filled her mouth and she would open her dark eyes, filled with strange anxieties.

With Luz Argentina, everything remained the same as when we met. When we moved into the neighbourhood, the Caicedo family was living in their two-storey house, with patios and fruit trees, so she always brought custard apples, guavas, oranges and lemons for mama. We were both black and she was my only close friend. After all, Margarita and Jaime Mann would look at us condescendingly whenever they returned from visiting their grandmother in the United States. My friendship with Luz Argentina was as lasting as if we had known each other from before we were born. I would fix lunch with her whenever mama had taken medication which prevented her from wetting herself. While she peeled the potatoes, I would iron the Mann's sheets. Only someone who has not had a sibling would understand why I loved her so much. She not only took away my loneliness; she was also my judge, my adviser, my joy, my informant and my companion at parties. At times she looked at me fleetingly, with a mixture of candour and reproach when I made a mistake with the words of a song. I used to comb her black hair and I taught her to put on eye make-up. On Friday nights my house was hers, my parents hers, my books, my dresses, my sanitary pads, my jewellery, my skirts, all hers. We spent time reading, talking about some girl, and about university. She was studying literature and I, jurisprudence. We talked about the professor who was having an affair with a student, about the strikes that were paralyzing the country and about the clients at the beauty salon where I worked. Manolo would allow me to leave early to go to classes. While we talked about our friends, Luz Argentina watched soap operas. At times I saw her as a little girl, capable of laughing about trivial things and crying for foolishness. She would get up and with long steps she would walk from side to side, barely talking in a strange voice. Perhaps the soap operas reminded her of her divorced parents. Then she would fall into deep silence and then burst out laughing at herself.

Nothing could tell us that fire, air, water, age, violence and all that festered in the heart would destroy a friendship that went so far back. Our intimacy went beyond knowing the days when we were menstruating, the colics I suffered or the erotic dreams that wet our pyjamas, the jokes exchanged at dusk, the flattery that made us blush, the labels that the boutique placed on local dresses to be sold as foreign items, the secrets of Manolo's bedroom, the threats from the Banco El Porvenir to those with overdue loans, the conquests of Jaime Mann who changed girlfriends every month.

Now her memory loomed large in my mind. I evoke her image with a desire to embrace her, to tell her that my house is still hers, my dresses also, my books, my earrings, my sanitary pads. Now we have forgiven life for the past evil which it did to us.

Susana fixed her blouse which was exposing her navel. Her grandmother, Matilde Congo, cut it small so that a little precious stone could be put into it, as if she knew that years later a man would adorn it with a diamond. She had inherited from her grandmother her flat nose and kinky hair. From her she learnt that she had been born in the Year of the Dog, that as an adult she would have romantic conflicts and according to the African Horoscope, her sign was the Wind. Her long practice of midwifery made her believe in destiny and she declared that babies born head first would lead a normal life but would be mediocre; those who came into the world with a caul came to serve God; those who were born bottom first would be successful in their professions and loyal; and those who came feet first would harbour deep hatred. Matilde used to say that her granddaughter was a special case because she arrived covered with filth shining like gold, which meant triumph, a happy life and that she would sleep like the dead. Years later, Marvin surprised her with legs bared, showing her private parts.

When Susana was born, her grandmother measured her umbilical cord. Four fingers made a knot, another four fingers, a loop and left another four so that she would be tall as the palm trees of Plenilunio. She applied hot fat, wrapped her like a mummy so that she would not have a big belly as a woman and passed her to Carlota to breast feed her. When the mother saw how greedy her daughter was she exclaimed: "I swear never to have another one." And she kept her promise as Susana was the only child of Carlota Montes and Joelí Garcés.

Joelí realized that it was better to go off to the city where his grandfather Mateo was the owner of a house bequeathed by doña Ofelia Seminario de Pino, the richest cocoa farmer in the region. The house was located on the embankment in front of Las Acacias Park. At first he panicked about leaving his homeland. He had felt the same way when he was pursued by a tiger that evening when he was chasing a partridge. Then he was ten years old but he remembered it as if it were yesterday. He moved about between the trees and a heavy breathing made him turn around. The fright was overwhelming. He wanted to run but he thought it would be better to behave calmly. He walked until he distracted the animal, then in one jump he climbed a tree. The furious tiger looked at him from below, strolled around the trunk and shook it with his body. For two days they remained in the same spot, watching each other. The tiger fell asleep but, from time to time, would raise his head to look at him. Joelí, tired of waiting for the spotted one to go away, climbed to the highest point of the tree from where he wished his father to see him and come and rescue him. "He has to come, he has to come," he said two hundred times. His father appeared accompanied by three hunters. They killed the animal and took the skin to adorn Joelí's bedroom floor – a recipe to help him overcome his fear of those animals.

Joelí installed himself in the residence, which was doña Ofelia's, and after living there for fifteen days he could not resist the temptation of taking a woman into his bed. He waited until nightfall so that no one would see her; and so he became the most popular ladies' man in the Barrio Alegre. For two months he had a different woman every night. One of them taught him to play chess and another to play the *guitarra* as she felt that a party lover should know how to play an instrument.

One morning as he was walking along the waterfront a Japanese offered him a job as a rower to go up the river in search of places where oil could probably be found. Miguel Aguas would be the pilot, as he knew all the rough parts of the river. Miguel was a heavily built black man who had grown up going up and down the river. They set out at dawn, taking advantage of the freshness when the tides seemed covered with foam. After sailing all day they docked in a bay. Kimoto pitched his tent and after taking photos, he lay down to study the plans and maps which he had carried. Meanwhile, his assistants took advantage of the break to bathe, wash their clothes and lie in the grass. Kimoto prepared his equipment and with the help of the assistants drilled holes in different places. From one he extracted a thick liquid which he put in a barrel, to which he attached a label with the date, place and quantity extracted. They spent the days extracting samples and throwing them in other barrels, going up the river, eating fresh fish caught by hooks hanging from the stern. They continued the expedition for one more month and when the canoe was overloaded they planned their return. With two more days to go for the expedition to end, the Japanese lay down naked on the grass, fascinated by the landscape, and began to give thanks to the eternal Ko Ko Ko, he said. He experienced peace and joy inside.

The night before completing the expedition they threw a *fiesta*. Kimoto took photographs and from a box he took twelve bottles of a liqueur made from sixty flowers and proposed a toast to the success of the expedition, the enchantment of the landscape, the moon, the pureness of the air, the river of clear waters, and to Okio, his financée whom, on his knees, he had promised to marry. Joelí spoke about the woman who taught him to play chess, Juana Charcopa. He toasted the one who taught him to play the *guitarra* and the ones who taught him such and such a position. Next Miguel urged everyone to drink to women even though they paid badly. He classified them as tall, small, fat, slim, dry and juicy. And he said that he thought about Irene Campás. The natives improvised a bongo and a drum and began to dance.

The Japanese jumped like an automatic device without paying attention to the beat of the music since he said he carried his rhythm inside. They drank until the bottles were empty and the young chacalaca birds announced daybreak. They collected their belongings and tried not to leave tracks. It occurred to Mr. Kimoto that others could have followed their tracks and would try to reveal the deposits. Staggering, they set off. The canoe sailed along, pushed by the current. The rowers felt the effects of the sixty flowers and while the boss rested, they began to dream of being in the arms of some hot-blooded mulatto and so they did not realize that the boat was capsizing. When they felt the collision they woke up. They had fallen in different positions. On opening his eyes Miguel saw vegetation he had never before imagined. The water was ice cold and clear. The fish and stones had another dimension. They made him want to remain there forever but he floated, and when he reached the surface he saw that Kimoto was sinking and grabbed him by the belt. Joelí threw them a raft, they hugged it, then they were rescued by three peasants one kilometre down the river. The accident changed the Japanese's plans and he forever renounced the search for the Devil's Shit. Years later in a gesture of gratitude Kimoto took one of Miguel's daughters to the United States.

Carlota Montes arrived in search of Joelí and as she did not find him she installed herself in the Puerto Bella Vista in the company of a village woman from Plenilunio where she was born. One night Joelí Garcés told her about his feelings in detail. He sang her three *boleros* to the beat of the *guitarra* and promised her eternal love. On the day that Joelí did not go to sing to her, she sent her godfather with a love note to the school where he worked as janitor which said, "I accept you as a husband." They got married with the consent of Matilde Conga and from then she learnt to take care of the house. When he fell ill, Joelí felt afraid of leaving her as a widow; cholera gave him the face of death. She decided to go to Ruth Mann, who lived on the corner from her house, to seek a job as a washerwoman.

Carlota learnt the good taste with which Ofelia Seminario had kept her house, which became a meeting place for her friends, the only property which she retained after the arrival of the 'Witches' broom' and the disaster of the 'Great Cocoa'. Doña Ofelia married a millionaire from the region, Manuel Pino, a union which made them enjoy life like perpetual single people. They met on the high seas on a trip around the world. The house had the marks of the past, hidden scars, wounds which the years opened up to them. However, the new owners changed a panel here and there, painted a wall, applied pepper to the corners to prevent woodworms and mitigate its old age. Susana took her classmates to meet her and she took their breath away. She lit the lamps, the wall lights and the chandeliers although the sun was still in its zenith because that was how doña Ofelia operated. When Joelí and Carlota's daughter turned fifteen they threw a *fiesta* which began at three in the afternoon and the guests did not leave until they were completely exhausted; a type of endurance contest.

It was the first time that Susana received a bouquet sent by a stranger. From then, every Friday the flowers arrived and created in her a growing affection for the mysterious admirer. And so the Garcés girl grew up committed to that man of her dreams. He shared her joys, her hopes and she sang of love for him and to him. On moonlit nights she imagined him as tall, black, with a dreamy smile and then she felt his fingers run across her body. The flowers arrived at any time on Friday like a handsome ghost which came to rest his lips on hers. She was resolved to marry whoever was sending those love messages made of flowers. That must be a man of extraordinary qualities, as he knew the key to tenderness, she told herself. That is why one Friday when the flowers did not arrive, she suffered a crisis which made her lock herself in the bathroom and when the sun set she discovered that the bouquet was on the porch of her house.

Around that time Joelí received a letter from Mr. Kimoto in which he informed him that he, Okio and his son Kimo were living in the United States and had many friends in Latin America. One day he would return with his family but not to sail that river. Another piece of correspondence almost gave him a heart attack, since it was a postcard signed by Ofelia Seminario de Pino, written with shaking hands. It was the first bit of information indicating that she was still alive but he preferred to hide the message since everyone in the house thought that she was resting on the other side. One month after receiving news of Ofelia, a postcard signed by the widow of Pino arrived. They cried unceasingly until they learnt the truth. Dawn found them at the Registrar of Properties and while the employee leafed through the books, Joelí covered his mouth with a handkerchief for it was filling with thick saliva. Carlota opened her eyes as if she were an owl. The clerk climbed up and came back down with books from 1911; he searched two or three times, without finding any copies of the deeds. They regretted believing that they were owners of the mansion. They had lived a mistaken reality. They had not made any effort to build their own house because they believed they had one for life. Joelí, after the honeymoon, carried his wife to the supposed house of his grandfather Mateo, previously converted into a brothel, but Carlota understood Joelí's weaknesses when he was single. He blamed Carlota's magic for him being a faithful husband. For her it was easy, since she had learnt to break in horses in Plenilunio.

The clerk, affected by the couple's anxiety, shouted, "Eureka!" He had found the copy of the deed signed by Ofelia Seminario whereby she had given the two-storey house located on the corner of Malecón and las Acacias to Mateo Garcés. Now they cried with joy and wet the document.

When Carlota's stepfather died, her mother, Matilde Conga, went to live with them. She arrived saying that her husband had died because of stupidity since with one enema of camomile and lemon he would have survived. Her granddaughter Susana was five years old at the time, and every night she would tell her stories. Her voice rang out through the shadows but at times only a whisper could be heard. Her grandmother extracted her first milk tooth with a piece of thread wrapped around the root; amidst screams and a promise that the rat would bring her money, she pulled it out with a tug.

Matilde resumed the habit of making 'balls' for breakfast. She brought the wide stone and the hand stone and would crush boiled banana, adding cheese or crackling to it. She never got accustomed to bread; she said it made people lose their memory.

Grandma said that she never knew which of the masters impregnated her because the first one to force himself on her was Carlos, the owner of the plantation, and then a few days later his son did the same, both times in the hills when she was picking cocoa. That is why she decided to give her daughter the surname Montes, although for her the surname Conga was the more powerful – one she had inherited from her mother. And since Carlos was the name of both father and son, she gave her the name Carlota.

Matilde, who was convinced that she could see the face of Shango in the sky, would sit on the balcony in the evenings and gaze at the heavens. It was she who taught Susana to believe in destiny; she said it pursues one like a hunting dog, sniffing until it finds its prey. She would say: "We have a guardian angel on whom we must call when we are in danger because he protects us." In time, Susana realized that the stories told by grandma were the product of her imagination and only when she learned to count did she begin to count them and ended up with nine hundred and six. She regretted not having written them down, to publish them some day. When Matilde started to suffer from colic, Carlota would apply suction pads. She refused to go to the doctor, maintaining that, "The only sickness is old age; the rest is rubbish."

She was born north of Plenilunio in a place where people used to give nicknames in the augmentative to men and in the diminutive to women. As her husband's name was Luis, they called him Luchón; a friend, Miguel, was nicknamed Miguelón; another who had swollen cheeks as a result of certain baths, was called Mejillón; the tallest man was known as Altón; the smallest woman was called Chiquitita; the fattest woman, Gordita; and the Albas women, Albitas.

One morning grandma made a hole in the patio, lit a coal fire in it, threw in medicinal herbs and then climbed into it. Everyone thought that grandma needed a straitjacket. Carlota and Susana begged her to stop such madness but she stayed in there. Her relatives kept watch next to Matilde who looked like an animal being roasted. She said that that was the penance she was paying for having eaten so much in life. At dawn she came out of the oven; when her granddaughter wanted to give her a hand, she jumped out like a hare. She went at once to clean the house, she brought water from the river and filled the barrels, she washed the Mann's clothes and ironed them. That night, she threaded her needle with a firm hand and while she mended Joelí's shirts she repeated these verses to her granddaughter:

When I caught smallpox,
I climbed up to heaven's door,
There I met my father
and also saw my grandfather
There were the hooks
That I took
When I went fishing
And there waiting to kill me
was the smallpox.

Later when Susana was ten years old and would go to Margarita and Jaime Mann's house to play, Matilde got the impression that the future of her granddaughter should be tied to theirs. Her argument was, "One marries one's neighbour."

This idea went round and round in her head, but it was absurd to think that a wealthy white man with eyes like a cat would fall in love with a poor black woman like her granddaughter. She remembered that Susana had been born under the sign of Scorpio in the Year of the Dog, one Friday at eleven at night, when there was a high tide, strong winds from the hill, a full moon and amidst the meowing of cats. These three signs were united in her granddaughter: Dog, Scorpion and Wind. The result was unbridled love. Not only did she believe it but she said to herself, "May Shango spare my life to see it!"

One evening, from the balcony, she saw a huge cloud of smoke which she took as a sign that she should leave the city. She was on the verge of crying out of sadness; that the ball of smoke would reach the heart of Shango. She went to her room, wrapped her belongings in a sheet and said, "I'm leaving."

However, two years later she returned, with the same bundle of things and installed herself in the same bedroom. Carlota and Joelí smiled. They knew she would soon leave. Before a week had passed grandmother and granddaughter resumed their stories and conversed for long periods. She reminded her about the guardian angel – it was to this angel that Susana prayed that Friday when it was full moon. Grandma showed her that she could leave her body and ascend to the planets through thought to converse with Shango, to look for the things she liked most, to live with them, to be them. She taught her to caress herself every night four fingers below the navel because that was where she would find energy. That night grandma left the iron out in the night air and at dawn she smashed her granddaughter's chest. "Instead of breasts you will have buds," she told her.

Susana learnt then that there was no guilt and that sin was invented by slave masters to torment the slaves. Matilde taught her that Santa Barbara was Shango, Jesus Christ was Obatala and that Yemayá was the goddess of the seas and rivers. Grandma kept visiting the house. Each time she came with less luggage. When she returned Susana was filled with joy. She took on the task of helping to wash the Mann's clothes. While she soaped up Ruth's dresses she remembered Mrs. Mann's uncle, a black man with a pronounced forehead, the one they called Frentón, who sold oranges in the market. Carlota took advantage of the opportunity to apply the ointment which had been prescribed for her rheumatism, but Matilde would tell her that she was suffering in vain for she could be cured with stinging nettle water.

At nights grandma would go to Susana's bedroom, lie next to her with her eyes closed and would mentally leave her body on the bureau to observe it as it aged. At times her granddaughter would hear her say, "You are becoming hunchbacked." Then she would re-enter her body and move here and there with a broomstick on her back to correct the hump. She taught her granddaughter things that would serve her throughout life and Susana became more and more accustomed to her grandmother's presence. The two would remain on the terrace and while Susana played the *guitarra,* Matilde would remain still as if she were praying that her granddaughter would be a good guitarist. At times they would do a duet and her granddaughter would laugh on listening to the words of her songs. Then the old woman would tell her fantasy stories. She would wake up at five in the morning and Susana would listen to her repeating um, um, um which came from the depths of her stomach and slowly rose up to her mouth. The um would continue for about twenty minutes and her voice would resound like a canon. The young girl gradually learnt to imitate her.

She left one Friday when on opening the door to the hallway she found a bouquet of dreams, the day that she sensed that a wealthy white man with a calm, kind, relaxed love, loved her granddaughter but that her granddaughter deserved much more. "It's a mistake," she said. Nobody knew what she was talking about. That day she went away because she did not want to be witness to the path that Susana's life would take, a path from which it would be impossible to escape.

They had been married for three years; yet Carlota had not conceived. Joelí proposed a trip to Matilde's farm. Early one morning they set off at high tide. Along the way she recognized each bend, she knew the scent of each plant, the places they grew and the insects that attacked them. She had made that trip many times by canoe and on foot, so it was easy for her to know where they were going but it was difficult for her to fight with the memory of the poverty which the people had to endure, the anguish of not having anything, the uncertainty of having something to eat. When she reached don Carlos' hill, she changed her position. She recognized the smell of cow dung. She had earned some sucres taking the landowner's cattle to drink water. She remembered bathing next to the cows. She must have been about twelve years old. She remembered the exact number of animals. There were fifteen under her care and she would take them five by five. She became quiet and remained seated there between the odours floating in the atmosphere.

The canoes went up and down laden with bananas, oranges, pears, custard apples, palm trees, papayas. Carlota inhaled the smell of wet earth with delight. She looked like a mare in heat. The peasant women washed their clothes in tubs and waved their hats in response to her greeting while Joelí shouted "Hey!" At midday they reached the house of the midwife Dominga, a woman who only spoke on full moon nights. They spent the night with her and when the river reflected the outline of the mountain, they continued their journey to Plenilunio. Carlota put aside her childhood memories to concentrate on the countryside which the moon presented when it smiled on the river. Joelí raised the paddle and pointing to a light which moved at great speed shouted, "There goes the *Riviel*."

He was referring to the legend of the doctor who in the 17th century was killed by his wife's lover while he was holding a lamp. He fell into the river and drowned, and now he walked the earth in search of a grave. When they arrived Matilde was talking with a toucan. She was happy for the arrival of the couple. Joelí and Carlota walked along the path which separated the palm trees from the mango trees. They sat on the grass, stayed there looking at the stars, inhaling the perfumed air of the flowers while they concentrated on the conception of a daughter. Joelí saw one of the constellations; it formed two S's and in those letters he looked for the name of his daughter.

"Susana," he said.

Carlota smiled. The journey had only one aim – to conceive a child in the open field, looking up at the sky, listening to the tomcats fight over the love of a female cat. She felt the wind on her body and asked her husband not to take off his hat or his shoes – the infallible formula for conceiving a daughter. Joelí caressed her breasts to concentrate on Carlota's exuberant body but he couldn't understand why he remembered Juana Charcopa, the woman who taught him how to play chess, and the no less exciting black woman who played the *guitarra*. Perhaps because Carlota was the synthesis of the women he loved.

When Carlota felt the urge to eat rose petals, she knew she was expecting a daughter. Then Joelí gave her a jewel which he found on Ofelia Seminario de Pino's night-table.

Carlota remembered her daughter's childhood days. Her memory expanded like a fan upon recalling days when she went to the bedroom where Susana was complaining of measles, fright, malaria and illnesses which left her in bed for several days. Her mother took her pulse and put her ear close to her chest. Everybody in the house was quiet. They walked on tiptoe, attentive to what the little girl said. Carlota, seated on her bed, breathed deeply. The girl heard her breathing while she counted rosary beads. Incense saturated the room.

The parents went to the window to look at the river while they talked. Joelí caressed Carlota's shoulder. They did not look anguished. They were thinking of returning to the country to keep Matilde's company when their daughter got married. Susana was the centre of their thoughts. They were generous enough to forgive and forget her mistakes.

She was preoccupied with her law studies, her work in Manolo's beauty salon and her neighbour, Luz Argentina Caicedo. Susana, the seed brought from Plenilunio, which would be the miraculous tree of magic fruit. They never imagined that their beloved daughter would fall into sin. When they woke up, their only thought was their daughter who had grown up with them. Their lives had value for and because of her. When Carlota prayed for children, unconsciously she was praying for her. When she prayed for the madwoman in the town, she was praying for her daughter. When she asked for health for the sick, she was asking for Susana. After finding out the facts, although she no longer believed in her and had lost the ability to judge her, she took her with her. In spite of this, she smiled, as if she was saying with her lips that she still loved her. Perhaps she would have been willing to forgive her if she had robbed, killed or committed libel – but for such a grave error, never.

The home of the Manns was located on the corner of the Malecón and Las Acacias Street, thus named because to the front there was a park where trees of that species grew. The park was enclosed by iron rails brought from Germany. In the centre there was a raised platform where the town's band played on Sundays. The Mann's house was a relic built by an engineer with the surname Rohng, who had fallen into disgrace because of the Black List during the Second World War. He was imprisoned along with his compatriots in a concentration camp in Texas City in the United States. The house was made of wood from Perú. The property had five bedrooms, all suitable for hanging hammocks for taking afternoon naps when the sun was hottest, or at night when the river celebrated its high tides. In addition there was a living room which overlooked the courtyard, planted with palm trees and two avocado trees. In the background there was a honeycomb, which suggested that the previous owners had romantic conflicts – since with the honey from the bees they would have been able to ward off impotence.

The house, abandoned for a long time, became a cave for rats. When Marvin and Ruth acquired it they painted it white. They lived there with their two children for ten years then they contracted an architect to remodel it and add a third floor. Margarita asked for a balcony to be added so that she could go out onto it and give thanks for the serenades. Ruth insisted on a green house to cultivate orchids, since she had read that Grace Kelly had a passion for that flower. Jaime wanted a tennis court to play with his friends and Marvin suggested building a terrace from where he could gaze at the surrounding landscape. On saying this, cold sweat wet his shirt since in his insomnia he had had a vision in which he was murmuring the name of Susana Garcés without realizing that that creature had introduced herself in the gaps of his memory and he called her at any hour. Requesting the construction of the terrace was like disclosing a trace of madness. At times he would get up barefooted to ask the Virgin Mary to do a miracle of putting his lips on those of that little girl since he knew that thoughts produce actions.

The decision to build the terrace even though Marvin thought that his wife would reject the project, was unanimous. That place would be his observation point to continue thinking about Susana. He would see her long legs like a filly, her almond-like breasts, her eyes like a rabbit and her plaits which fell around her head. He would be alone with her even if it were from a distance. He would have her as near as if he were touching her. He suggested the terrace with such confidence that to Ruth it seemed like a natural request for him to get the breeze as he read his newspapers and magazines, and to look at the countryside of the estuary and the hills since she had noticed that lately he was rambling on in verses.

Marvin approved the budget for the work on condition that the remodelling begin with the terrace. Later when he mentioned this to Susana she did not believe it. As soon as the remodelling started and the cement smell had disappeared, invitations were issued to celebrate the opening. Ruth ordered dishes learnt in Paris and invited the authorities, the Ambassador of the United States, her husband's country of origin, the French Ambassador, because she had lived for many years in Paris, and her mother-in-law so she could come to advise her son who, instead of showing signs of maturity behaved like a young man of twenty. Marvin got up early at five to do gymnastics following the manual of Charles Atlas. After bathing and dressing he recited poems and excerpts from romantic novels. He put on his pants in one jump, developed after two years of practice. He had an obsession for separating himself from the world of the handicapped. At fifty-two years of age, he still wore the haircut of twenty years ago, with a fringe which hid the little grey hairs. He covered his blue eyes with dark glasses so that the sun would not accentuate the wrinkles and he used Cologne 4711 – that way he prepared himself for the eventual encounter with Susana. In the beginning he did not think that his thoughts of the Garcés girl would last, but with the passing of time there was no way of erasing it, and the older he became the more his passion for her intensified.

Ruth served him breakfast in the sunroom, which served as the everyday dining room surrounded by ornamental plants and mirrors. He almost always ate the same thing. The only thing that varied was the juice – sometimes apple, orange or grapefruit. He refused green orange because according to him it fermented in the stomach. He mixed whole wheat bread with low fat cheese and he added a tablespoonful of granola to yoghurt. He never forgot to take his capsule of lecithin, and at midday he took calcium and magnesium, recommended by a friend to prevent arthritis. At lunchtime he ate only herbs. Afterwards he lay in his hammock to read the newspaper headlines. He focused on economic topics. Then on the wings of Susana's memory he would sleep for half an hour and then go to the bank. In his office he had a calendar with the picture of a young black girl who carried a bouquet of illusions.

He examined the loan applications which his daughter Margarita selected. On Thursdays the Board of Directors would meet to discuss the happenings of the week and approve or reject loans. Then he would recline in an armchair to remember the time when his children played basketball in the yard with Susana. He would smile on seeing her jump and bend her waist. She was dressed in a short skirt which revealed white underwear with lace. He applauded her when she 'basketed'. The girl would look at him with the shyness of her nine years. Afterwards he invited them to have a cold drink and while they savoured it, everyone laughed. When it rained the children bathed in the open air under the *canoeras*.

On vacations Marvin would take the children on rides in the car and go as far as the port. Then the three would run along the beach, play tag, draw castles in the sand with bridges, towers, walls, stairs, gardens, passages and rooms. They made Chinese labyrinths. Jaime and Susana imagined walking through them and getting lost, finding no exits. Quiet, they would look pensively at each other, only concerned about finding the exits. Tired, they lay down in the sand and Jaime draped one leg over Susana's body while Margarita entertained herself making little paths with the remains of seashells and Marvin refreshed himself with the breezes and with the smiles of children.

From the day he saw Susana in a bathing suit which revealed her budding breasts, he understood that she would soon be a young lady and in the course of their impossible love he followed her growth step by step. On Saturdays he was punctual for playing chess and lived delicious moments on getting a glimpse of Susana.

Because Marvin had inherited his parents' religion, every Sunday he went to church along with his brother José. His father, Federico Mann, born in New York, took the opportunity for his children to read the Bible aloud. He loved this verse: "He who has much anger will suffer, if you use violence, it will bring new evil." Marvin never forgot it and it became a part of his life. His mother, Mary Clarke, born in Buffalo and educated in New York, belonged to the Sunday Choir. When she was a girl, she learned to play the piano and then went to the conservatory. Marvin inherited her sensitivity, hence evening after evening he wrote verses. His height of one metre eighty-six was inherited from his father, and since both parents had blue eyes, his children also had them. Federico belonged to the distinguished society against cancer and for this reason he did not allow smoking in the house. Besides that, he attended the Fishing Club, and he almost always went walking in the south of the city where the river ran, washing the fields. Mary used the occasions to take her children on a picnic – which they loved because they would eat fresh fish.

When Mary came to visit, Margarita and Jaime had a *fiesta* because their grandmother brought them toys, puzzles, sweets and sports clothes. They had fun and talked with her. She would open her photo album for them and tell them the story of each of her children; but she had already forgotten who was the baby lying in the chamber pot or crawling across the carpet, since her memory was slipping.

Federico Mann built the house where Marvin and José were born and spent their infancy. First he made the façade on a cartridge paper and then designed the bedrooms and living room. Mary wanted a big, well ventilated kitchen because she spent a good part of the day making dough for pastries. When Federico worried about her fatness, he prohibited her from entering the kitchen and kept her on a diet of fruits and warm water. He detested fat women. It was the only time the children heard them disagree. From then Mary became afraid of sweets and siestas; because of that she sometimes dozed off in the rocking chair.

For Federico, the most difficult thing was building the spiral staircase. He designed it twenty times but the levels were not equal. He would begin enthusiastically and in the middle of the project he would realize the error of his calculations. He could not explain the hidden causes, and they prevented him from continuing without suspecting that he would meet his death on it years later. One day he was at the point of abandoning his project when it occurred to him to assemble it from top to bottom and it worked that way. The house turned out to be big. Marvin and José played chess after dinner in the basement.

Almost within one month of living in the area they planted

four apple trees and two cherry trees. The men dug the holes and Mary put in the plants. After a while they acquired a Great Dane. Marvin, enamoured, watched him eat since he ate ten pounds of meat, drank two jugs of water and a pot of barley. He would go out to the gate and urinate on the post. They never heard him bark. They all thought he suffered from paralysis as he only opened his mouth to eat. One night there was a stench. Frightened, Mary locked him in her bedroom. The next morning the dog was dead.

Marvin's parents' house was located on the outskirts of New York City on the lands of a rancher who decided to urbanize the property. In the beginning when Federico built the house, he suffered anxieties because of the absence of basic facilities. His wife made a very detailed shopping list since if he needed anything he had to go searching for many miles, which is why there was a general mobilization in the house. But on seeing that the Manns had moved to that place, other people came and build their homes there too, and they always remembered that the Manns had been the pioneers and for that reason they always respected and appreciated them.

Mary Clark, who played the organ for the church choir, crossed the door at exactly ten forty-five. One day Federico dared to shake her hand and tell her that she was the reincarnation of Beethoven. Mary looked at him. The compliment meant a lot. Nobody imagined that in her later life, the famous musician had been the inspiration for her happiness. They did not understand the absurdity of her children's destiny. José, who from childhood had shown an ability for numbers, dedicated himself to the study of exact sciences and one afternoon they heard him scream. He had discovered that the square did not have four equal sides as mathematicians claimed. He thought he would die from the excitement about his discovery since this would revolutionize the world of science. The most absurd thing about the situation was that his parents did not understand their child's theory. In reality they understood his words but they were not able to understand the ideas he expressed. They admired José's talent when even with laryngitis he tried to explain to them in his notebook that $A^2= L^2i-d=1V^2$. His parents, however, shook their heads as a sign that they did not understand. Then José said, "As of tomorrow I will give you classes in mathematics; I need to be understood."

Federico and Mary's concern was Marvin, who did not show any maturity despite his being 23 years old. He would stroll through the garden reading until sunset. Three times per week he went to a Spanish course but it was impossible to know what he was planning. On Mary's suggestion, he abandoned his love for books of the previous century, and instead subscribed to a literary magazine. After a year of overwhelming readings, he participated in a poetry competition with the hope of winning the first prize, which he didn't. He slept very little in order to learn to write like the famous poets, which was why he walked around more asleep than awake, and at times would talk to himself since in his house he was not allowed to refer to anything that was not reality. Twice he assumed the role of Don Quijote; he went to the poor areas to give away toys and sweets to black children.

One day he decided to send his "Ode to the Horse" to another competition. He won the second prize and had to read it in public. He had dreamt so much about that moment that in one lyrical movement his false moustache, which gave him the appearance of Flaubert, fell off. Among those present were the members of the Horseback Riding Club, who created excitement and demanded the first prize for Marvin since they claimed that the poem was a valuable contribution to education and an example for men just as mares were for women. Marvin went home riding the horse given to him by the men of the Club. His parents could not believe what they were seeing and the neighbours looked out to see what was neighing.

"It's Marvin Mann," said an old man.

It never became clear which of his parents convinced Marvin to seriously earn a living, but Federico managed to see his son take his first step in the field of business; then he said he would die peacefully. He made him a small office in his study. He linked him to the world of banking, and Marvin adorned his office with a calendar which showed a young black girl with a bouquet of flowers, like a foreboding.

One afternoon when Federico descended the spiral staircase he felt dizzy and went tumbling downstairs. The years had taken away his agility and if he had thought about old age he would not have built that type of stairs. Too late. Mary heard the thud, went to see what was happening and her eyes became cloudy when she saw her husband lying in a pool of blood and breathing like a fish that had been taken out of water. Panic paralysed her and weeping was her refuge on seeing that her happiness was coming to an end.

Two years after Federico's death, Marvin packed his suitcase and went to fulfil his lifelong dream to discover South America. He never imagined that when he turned fifty he would fall in love with a black girl.

But on learning about his plans, his mother begged him on her knees not to go to those countries. She had read in a magazine something about the existence of a savage tribe called 'Aucas' which devoured whites.

"Do it for your father's bones," she begged him.

Marvin fixed his compass and left for Paris. Mary withdrew her savings for her obedient son and gave him her blessing. After five months of spending his energies in cabarets, one morning as he walked along the streets of Paris he saw soldiers in a plaza marching to the beat of a band. He became enthusiastic about the martial air. Never had he seen French soldiers march to the gander step. They played the Marsellaise before a courthouse. On hearing it as he arrived there, he felt something running through his veins. He put his hand on his heart and sang, not the Marsellaise, but his own national anthem. He followed the crowd, felt a shove, and instinctively looked for his wallet in all his pockets. The shock was great; it had disappeared. Discouraged, he did not know where to go. He tried to separate himself from the parade but the obstacles prevented him. Frightened, he thought of putting his fingers in someone's pocket. Imaginary fears stopped them. Soon he would finish the act. He made his way through the crowd. An official was raising the flag of France to the sound of the cornette. He put his hands in a spectator's pocket and was on the verge of jumping for joy; he had recovered his wallet! He retreated, agitated, thinking about prison and trembling. Then he lifted it to his chest and unable to contain his anxiety he kissed it several times and decided to leave the place. He checked the few dollars which remained, his mother's photograph and his friends' addresses.

He cried with joy and to celebrate his finding, at nightfall, he went to a nightclub called Delice; there he saw Ruth Sánchez. Her eyes were opaque from too much nightlife. She wore a short skirt. Her legs revealed black stockings with a diamond design. Marvin saw her walk and imagined she was South American. His intention on calling to her was to practise his Spanish. She smiled on hearing his language. Marvin did not know what to do in front of those eyes filled with sadness and a body with a fragrance of tenderness and death. He invited her to have a glass of wine. She only smiled. After the second drink they talked about the things of life. Drops of cold sweat ran down Ruth's forehead which she tried to hide. On a piece of paper, she begged him to take her from that place. For Marvin, that was a difficult task since she was not legal. She had come to the country on holidays. A woman named Irene Zander took her to take care of two children but she did not find the house of the family who required her services and so Irene employed her at the Délice. She had learnt French in the three years she had been away from her country. She exhaled and resolved not to let the young man escape.

It was on a hunch that she tried to save herself from drowning. Experience had taught her to read the features of the face and in Marvin's eyes she saw a poet. She confessed to him that in that place she felt diminished and while they were conversing she raised her glass to drink the last drops and was afraid she would hear something negative so she used modesty as a resource. Each of her words moved Marvin to compassion. He thoughtfully submerged himself in deep reflection. He saw her as fascinating. While he explained his plans to her, Ruth discerned the thoughts of the North American. The slow music played, inviting conversation and the consumption of liquor. From the bar, her friends saw her laugh. Marvin did not want to commit himself so he limited himself to listening; but she soon said, "I will thank you all my life."

He would wait for her outside, a block from the establishment. Ruth, pretending to go to the bathroom, went to the end of the corridor, emotions clouding her thoughts. Under the carpet she had hidden a large picklock stolen from a client, which she kept under strict custody for more than a year. It shone in the light. It made a soft sound in the keyhole. She grabbed the money that was hidden in a notebook, and which she had earned. Everything was in order; she didn't want to take anything else. She wanted to erase every memory that tied her to that place. She felt sad about not saying goodbye to her friends who had been her friends since her arrival at the nightclub. She thought about leaving them a note without explaining where she was going but her heart was full of doubts. She went towards the door. Soon she returned; she took the newspaper. In it was evidence of the time she had spent in Paris, her dreams, her pains.

She remembered two years ago she had slipped through a window and went to seek help from a florist. A man asked her what she wanted and she told him to escape from the nightclub.

The man telephoned and she thought it was to notify the police. Then immediately two bodyguards from the Délice property took her back to the establishment. She decided not to speak. She did not resign herself to forget what she had been; she should not adapt to that life. She passed in front of Irene without looking at her. She closed the bedroom door with the latch and waited until everyone was asleep. Irene deceived me into bringing me here as if I were a child. It has been so long and without any news of my parents, not even a word to say they are alive. My father did not like the idea that I was leaving them. It was true that I was coming to Paris to care for babies but my mother thought that in those lands our luck would change since my father had no job and my mother was selling food and rearing chickens in the yard.

You are right, Madam. Mothers always have a sixth sense. You will see that it is going to go well with Ruth. Let her go. And papa said, do not give permission for her to go; she is under age. Mama cried because she said that in this country there is no future, that the city has no drinking water, the streets are dusty, the flies and the quagmire, the worms. What hope was there for a pretty little girl like my Ruth? Irene agreed that she was right, that it was a shame to live in a town like that. So papa said, it's OK, where do I sign for my Ruth to go to Paris? I jumped with joy. I thanked him with a kiss on the forehead. Papa, you are the best father in the world. Mama cried with joy because her daughter Ruth would travel to Paris to meet other men and have someone to marry and improve her race. Here with these blacks, what hope is there, Miss Irene? It's better to take her, take care of her for me; don't let her get ill. Write and say how it is going.

I waited until everyone was asleep and I took half a bottle of sleeping tablets. I was feeling as if everything was disappearing and I was flying and I entered a world where everything was transparent. They found me unconscious, my hair was in disarray and the mattresses were on the ground. Irene gave me first aid and the doctor did the rest.

On leaving the bedroom, I could not believe it. I bumped into the concierge but I was undaunted because I was going towards freedom. In the next few minutes I managed to put on my hat and a client's coat. It was the only opportunity; I had waited for it for three years, two months and four days. I knew it because in that instant there was a neon calendar in the plaza. On the corner Marvin hugged me.

"I swear to love you all my life," Ruth told him.

Two months after they arrived in Bella Vista port, Ruth's parents died in a car accident. Marvin participated in a competition, this time not literary but as an aspiring manager in shipping.

Out of thirty participants he was the only one who answered several questions in verse and translated them into three languages since Ruth was his French teacher during the time that the trip lasted. The month Marvin assumed the position of manager of the shipping company he married Ruth as her pregnancy was beginning to show.

The wedding was a social event. She invited all the foreigners who lived in the city. She wore a white dress with a three-metre train and orange blossoms on her hands and asked Marvin that the day she died he should bury her like that in her wedding dress. After six months she gave birth and had a close brush with death since Margarita, the name with which they baptised the baby, was born feet first. She was the delight of her parents, the queen of the house, the community and the city. In the month of her birth she received hundreds of congratulations and two hundred dolls including those that said, 'Mama', 'Papa', 'I'm defecating'; they cried, they walked and they sang. As she took her first steps, Marvin bought a car to take her for rides. Three years later Jaime was born. Margarita looked at him as if she wanted to ask her parents why they were sharing everything with that intruder. She grew with the strange notion of discovering everything, knowing everything. She had felt indispensable from the time she was in her mother's womb. Very often she only needed to make a gesture in order to get her way.

Mama opened the window to let the breeze in since the heat was intensifying with the evaporation of the recent showers of rain. Rats, cockroaches and flies entered hurriedly in search of refuge. I remembered that when I was a girl I would have fun with Jaime, Margarita and Luz Argentina tying a cord to the neck of lobsters and running. We would make them fly like planes. We used to go from one house to another on rafts in the muddy waters. Inside the hut made of planks and palm leaves, I would feel Jaime's moist skin when he tickled me on my breasts then we would play mama and papa. He on my body and I asking him to get off because my stomach hurt under his weight moving up and down on me. I would say, "Jaime, leave me alone, get off now, I don't want to play anymore." Then we would cover ourselves with a sheet to listen to the song of the rain. Each drop had its own note and we would sleep until we heard mama's voice calling me. "Susana, come child, it's lunchtime."

I leaned over the balcony; the water was still stagnant. The drains could not lead it away and it formed ponds. Mama was applying a pomade to her hands, her arms, her knees. Nothing stopped her rheumatism. I went to iron the sheets and shirts of the Manns. Afterwards I heard a sigh like a noise in the branches – she had fallen asleep.

I lowered the volume on the transistor since her rest was a most sacred thing. She had put her hands on her chest and a blanket covered her legs. I admired her vigour for her work and the strength with which she bore the pains of her illness. When papa was ill with cholera, for fifteen days he was delirious with fever on his forehead and loose bowels. Then she understood the obligation of earning a living with her hands. She went to Ruth Mann's house and got the job to iron and wash all the family's clothes. The work filled her face with smiles. She felt morally responsible for our destiny. When papa got a salary increase she didn't give up her job and made us understand her right to use her time in her way. She washed from eight in the morning until two in the afternoon then she went to the kitchen. She almost never changed her routine. When I was at home, she warned that she would keep long hours of silence. That way I would not be next to her but it was as if her spirit was protecting me and even though she did not like my dances or my songs and censured my screams, she was the image of my conscience. I, her pride and she, the invisible presence in my blood. She prepared chocolate and cheese for dessert with roasted plantain and served it with something salt. For her, preparing a meal was a ritual: On Mondays, she made barley rice soup, so that there would always be money in the home, and shrimp and guava sweets. On Wednesdays, puree of pumpkin and roasted meat. On Thursdays, trotters broth and *muchines* of ripe plantain and cheese. On Fridays, fried fish with a lot of garlic and an onion sauce. On Saturdays, inevitably the cocoa, which had special significance as it reminded her of her grandmother. Sunday was God's day; she read the Bible and we went walking; we dined out on *cebiche* with banana chips and milk. Late at night she grated coconut and used the juice next day to make cassava bread for breakfast. Along with Grandmother Matilde, she created the family garden and in it they sowed lemon balm plants, mint, lemon verbena, aloe and parsley; all the old pots and tins served as flowerpots.

Sometimes I found her on the piles of clothes contemplating the sky as if she were praying before beginning the job. It was her habit to open the bundle of clothes with a ritual of humour, sweat and smells. She would bring each piece to her nose in three breaths – the first, short and quick, the second, slow and the last, deep. As a result, she knew the life and miracles of the Mann family. Ruth was capable of defending her home like a lioness.

Her dresses, brassieres, blouses and panties carried a smell of salt residue, inclined towards vanity and lies.

When mama washed her clothes, she chose a special soap to maintain her personality. Marvin's shirts carried the signs of a discreet man, mild character; his exhalations were of a calm person with large muscles, broad shoulders and a small deviation in his spine. He never complained about a badly washed pair of pants or a badly ironed shirt. He preferred pale colours, white tones with blue stripes. His fly showed that it was little used. He was very drawn to young people. On the other hand, Jaime's briefs bore evidence of stains from worldly pleasures; his shirts smelled of racehorses, cigarettes, whisky. He did not dress formally – red shirts, green, yellow, bright colours with pictures of monsters, singers and legends, his blue jeans with patches on the back and stained pockets. Because of the colour of his clothes, mama would say that he was capable of laughing even at his own shadow. Margarita wore short skirts, red, black and green stockings. She liked silk and knitted fabric. Her blouses had pronounced necklines. She didn't wear brassieres. She had small teasing breasts, a strong sense of humour was dominant and she tended to be serious and proud. Her breath was filled with Jean Naté but she exuded hatred. Mama could never explain why she felt anxiety whenever she washed the clothes of that little girl.

It was her habit to soak the pants, shirts, underwear, handkerchiefs in a large tub filled with water. She put them in and left them there for an hour. Then she sat to wash, folded her legs and gathered the dress between them. I would see her bend over, move her hands, first with force then gently; at times the foam would reach her face. While she scrubbed, hundreds of drops of sweat fell into the tub. She scrubbed the collars, the shirt cuffs; she wrung, swaying from side to side; she scrubbed the pants which at times came with mud and filth. I noticed that she was gradually becoming hunchbacked, but she attended to her work without fail. In the shade, behind the cords with hanging clothes, her face would emerge with the satisfaction of having won a victory.

Afterwards she would wash the sheets which the wind blew like flags. The following day she would wash the pillowcases, tablecloths, napkins and towels. At times she felt like she was falling over. When the sun was at its worst she moistened her forehead and took some sips. She did not whistle; she used to say that women had no right to pucker their mouths like dogs. She liked to listen to the trill of the birds. But I whistled when I urinated. If I did not whistle, I could not empty my bladder. I whistled proudly with my body leaning forward. It was one of my inviolable secrets.

It was her custom to read the Bible aloud, pronouncing each word correctly as if tasting them. On occasion she repeated the verses to learn them by heart. My throaty way of speaking and high-pitched laughter terrified her.

She never went to the cinema or the theatre. She was convinced that growing old poor was the worst punishment. She kept her salary for some months in a wooden box which she opened at the end of each month to count the money accumulated. Papa did not manage to convince her to put her savings in a bank. He warned her that when she least expected it, a thief could come along and carry off everything. And so, it happened months later. When for the first time I saw her count her money, batch the notes according to their value and put the obverse on top, I had the impression that she was living in fear and drew close to God out of fear of old age and hid her anxieties with prayers. She got up at five in the morning to read her Bible, look at the sky since she liked the clouds, then she would turn on the stove until the water heated, then she would go back to bed. I would hear her laugh with papa. They played like children.

Once she was alone she would hurry to take the nettle water which Grandma Matilde had brought her. For her, only Sunday was different. She would get ready early in her dress made of shantung silk; she would wear black patent leather shoes. She would splash on Florida water and smile as we left on papa's arms. We returned at nightfall; after the service we would go to the port. We almost always invited Luz Argentina. We talked about imaginary boyfriends and got goose pimples. We liked jogging to the other side of the beach; in the orange season we threw the peel behind us and they would fall in the design of some letter which, we would say, was the initial of the name of whoever we would marry. I always got M; from then I was sure that I would marry a Manuel, Medardo, Miguel, Manelao, Makarios. Luz Argentina's orange peel suggested that she would marry a man whose name began with K, but on finding no names with that initial, we laughed.

Before Grandmother Matilde arrived, I slept alone in my room and I bathed on the terrace; I collected a tank of rainwater, which was colder and purer than that from the river. From the terrace the flat roof of the neighbours' houses could be seen. Mama kept the walls of our terrace adorned with pots of geraniums. Besides, there was a table with two chairs and there I practised the *guitarra*, embroidered, did my chores and exercises. When I menstruated I had colic that punctured my ovaries; then I would turn down my bed. The wind made the pains less intense; my screams could be heard from afar. Luz Argentina's mother sent me a foreign remedy which made me sleep for two hours, but on awakening I would feel the stabs of pain with greater force.

When mama completed three years as washerwoman with the Mann family, she put on her Sunday dress, her patent leather shoes and went to speak with Ruth to ask her to file her Social Security since the ointment which she applied for rheumatism had doubled in price.

Ruth denied her request and mama came home sobbing. Within the month the lady of the house came to speak to mama since she had lost a very expensive foreign blouse. She told her that she was responsible and should pay her for it. The accusation forced mama to resign her job as washerwoman.

Marvin kept his desires a secret. He was in love with Susana but he felt that time was presenting something like a trap in his way. At nights he preserved his illusions with little prayers to the Virgin Mary. He set his binoculars to look at Susana to see her in her sky blue shorts doing her exercises. He would cry when he thought that he had lost her. At times he felt drained from not being able to confess his torment. His wife, Ruth Sánchez, had abandoned all hopes of making him give up his obsession with astrology since she was persuaded that his obsession was that science. Marvin spent complete hours looking at the sky. When he heard the neighing of some horse tied to a post in the park, he recited his "Ode to the Horse" then he would get up and write a sonnet for his Dulcinea. But Susana Garcés had fallen in the net of another love and Marvin saw her stroll through the gate holding the hands of a young man. Poetry was his refuge in which he emptied his effervescence. In the first month of Susana's romance with that stranger, he granted all the loans which he had pending without reading the reports which Margarita passed on to him – a promise made to the Virgin so that he would obtain Susana's love. One night he stayed up with his long-ranged view, observing the terrace of his beloved. Ruth brought him an infusion of lemon balm so that he could see Halley's Comet better.

The truth was that even though Marvin saw Susana in love with another man, he never lost faith that he would achieve his goal. He was sure that sooner or later he would have her in his bed and that obsession kept him alive. He purified his actions as an efficient way of gaining favour in the sight of the Virgin. His love for Susana made him cold in his relations with his wife. He had to conserve his strength for the possible encounters with Garcés. He thought that from one moment to the next he would receive notice of the trip of his rival and this reassured him greatly.

Ruth massaged his shoulders and he spoke to her about Edmund Halley, the English astrologer born in 1656 who died in 1742 – the discoverer of the comet which visits Earth every 76 years. His wife interrupted him,

"But if it has already passed, what are you looking at¿"

"The comet may appear suddenly."

During her years of marriage Ruth never doubted her husband's love. Now that their children were grown and he adored them, she had no reason to doubt his faithfulness. She devoted her time to the home and social commitments. In the afternoons she went to the Ladies' Club and on weekends to the supermarket with the entire family and to the Pyramid Centre where Marvin was a member. Never, as she was then, was she identified with her husband. Everyone knew her as Mrs. Mann and saw them as a couple without problems. At nights she met with her friends to play cards. They never got tired of repeating the saying that there was never a home as respectable as theirs. She insisted on telling her friends about the adoration that Marvin professed.

"If I started to disappear, Marvin would die."

During nights of loneliness, she comforted herself with the idea that her husband, a foreigner, had given her children with blue blood. She had discovered that blood was not only red – a theory she defended in many debates at the Red Cross, of which she was a member. Sometimes she declared on the radio and in the local newspaper that blood had several colours which determined intelligence. That is why whites were more intelligent than other races. Marvin could not get those absurd thoughts out of her head. Oh, my God! If Ruth has black relatives, where does she get all that pride from¿ he would ask himself. That is why she developed the habit of going out after five in the afternoon so as not to burn her skin.

When they were invited to have lunch in the open air, she

suggested installing a tent that would cover several metres around her table. Because of this one midday when she felt a tremor she did not leave the house. Ruth was in her best period; she had managed to install herself as President of the New Book Club and step by step she was becoming a factotum. She managed the funds of various institutions, made speeches and her photograph appeared in local weekly newspapers. She allowed her hair to grow, tinted it blonde, smooth and long to her waist. She always used mascara; she always embellished her eyes with blue colour contact lenses even though she did not need them.

One morning she dressed in an emerald necklace and blue velvet suit for a portrait. That was the photograph which the newspapers published when she celebrated another birthday. An outstanding foreign artist did her portrait in oil. She became a society queen, whose opinion on all matters was indisputable.

When she practised the speech which she would give on the Commemoration of the Day of the Race, she proposed, among other things, to record that she was the only woman in the country who had travelled across the Atlantic from Sweden to Finland and from there to England, where she had an interview with Queen Elizabeth II and she knew Paris like the back of her hand. Marvin, surprised, listened and wondered if it was the same woman he discovered in a nightclub.

When Marvin received the news that Carlota resigned her job, he awoke at five o'clock with a concern that made it difficult for him to breathe. The whole night he thought of going to Carlota to ask her to reverse her decision. It would give him an opportunity to squeeze Susana's hand or hold her in his arms like he used to do when she was a girl. He woke up with an emotional fever because he was in high spirits; he had taken his medication in the wrong order. While fasting he took two capsules of ginseng which according to the prescription should be taken after breakfast. His task was to persuade Mrs. Garcés that there was no one in the city or in the world who washed their clothes better than she or who left them as white and, above all, as fragrant since they carried the smell of the sun.

That is how Susana would smell, he thought. He was lying in the hammock until the clock struck six in the morning. He planned the interview step by step. He was so engrossed that he was not even aware that Ruth passed by his side naked with a green substance covering her body. He, with his power of conviction, would change Carlota's mind. He analysed the details, whispered expressions, gestures; he would not leave any stone unturned. The ginseng lifted his energies. The clothes ironed by Susana had the magical power to convert him into a dreamer; he seemed to be sleeping with her. My precious girl, come and he turned in the bed to look for her. The sheets had the ability to make his Little Rabbit appear. Embracing the pillow, he kissed her. My girl, my Susana, and he went off to sleep with his head on her. He changed his mind; instead of personally going to the home of the Garcés, he would send a simple letter asking them to forgive Ruth and telling them how the decision had disturbed him. On receiving the message, Susana would reply and that way they would establish a mode of ongoing correspondence which would result in him seeing her.

But since the time to go to the Garcés home had passed, he postponed his project for the following day and asked the Virgin to have compassion on him and give him luck. He wondered what reasons Carlota had for resigning from the job as washerwoman. He was willing to double her salary and give her a three-monthly bonus plus a monthly gift. The following night he slept dressed and took off his shoes because of a corn that had formed from the last pair of shoes that he had bought from a Turk, but between sleeping and waking he dreamt of the encounter. On hearing the washerwoman's rooster, he went to the bathroom. He had to face that challenge with bravery because his destiny depended on this visit.

Marvin was on the hunt for a reason – to see Susana. When he went to her house he was prepared to take the next step. He felt as if he had a fever and his body trembled. A woman with a peasant-like appearance opened the door; it was Matilde. The hall with planks of lignum vitae and the handrails made with balustrades impressed him with their beauty. On the landing there was a carpet with enough space for a flowerpot. From the ceiling hung two old lamps with eight lights and edges of gold. Matilde took him to the living room which displayed furniture from the past century. While he was being attended to, he remembered that the house had belonged to a rich cocoa farmer, Ofelia Seminario de Pino. He listened to Susana's voice singing a *bolero* accompanied by her *guitarra*, which was sufficient to make him feel more excited. Mr. and Mrs. Garcés appeared almost immediately. Carlota perceived the smell of Margarita's father and it seemed to her that something more than gratitude for her services had brought Marvin there because his mood seemed a bit different. She looked at his eyes and could not identify his feelings exactly. It occurred to her that Mr. Mann was in love.

Joelí was surprised by Marvin's visit. He was now the manager of the Banco El Porvenir as the shipping company dismissed him since no employee could understand the sonnets he wrote as reports. Susana, ignorant of what was happening in the living room, continued playing the *guitarra* and singing. He thought he was in paradise listening to heavenly music. He forgot why he had gone there but Matilde saved him by offering him a glass of orange juice with pieces of ice. As he sipped it, he told her about Vitamin C – it prevents colds; and without any clear direction in his conversation he talked and went from one topic to another.

Next they went on to talk about cassava bread and the way in which it was prepared and she offered him two pieces. He asked for another; he said he had never tasted anything like it. When he saw a chess set on a corner table, he went to look at it and learned that Joelí played the game with Carlota, so he promised to come at eight on Saturday nights to play. Next they talked about a black goddess named Baltasar, goddess of the seas of Angola and of the festival of the Black Mother without imagining that one day he would be living the emotions of that celebration taken by the arms by the daughter of Joelí and Carlota.

Susana paid attention to that voice with an accent she knew from her childhood when she played in the Mann's yard. Jaime! She said his name with emotion on remembering his blue eyes and his hands soaping her back and the tickles which he gave her nipples. She sharpened her ears to listen to the conversation. Joelí was convinced that he had survived many years of marriage because of chess. He recognized that it was the only thing that saved him from fornicating. Susana could not believe it; Jaime had come to her house. It was a miracle that God had done for her; she fell on her knees before the crucifix. He was her dream since she was a child; his scent was never erased. He had been her playmate but her grandmother, Matilde, on entering the bedroom told her that it was not Jaime but Marvin who was visiting them. She hated her mistake.

He returned on Saturday night at eight on the dot; he went to play a game of chess with Joelí. While they moved the pieces they helped themselves to grapefruit juice and remembered anecdotes of their past. The owner of the house told him that the Japanese, Kimoto, invited the daughter of Miguel Aguas to study in the United States. He called his wife to ask her the name of the young woman.

"Moconga. She's an athlete, black and full-bodied like her father."

Susana looked at him in the mirror; she thought to herself that she had never seen such blue eyes; it was as if she were looking at the sea with its blue dress. She was transfixed for a few moments, savouring that small landscape; unconsciously she made the V for victory sign with two fingers and exclaimed, "What a beast!"

She went to her bedroom but those eyes followed her and when she went back to playing the *guitarra*, she carried her hands to her head because she couldn't decide if those eyes which followed her were Marvin's or Jaime's.She didn't sort out her confusion but she was sure she was in love with one of the two. Accepting this ambiguity, she entered an obsessive world in which there was no separation, jealousies or reproaches, where she could enjoy herself without regrets or meanness.

She remembered that her grandmother had taught her that sin was an invention of the slave owners; they created it to facilitate their control over the slaves. The idea of being indiscriminately in love horrified her, but those calming and welcoming eyes had a subjugatory power, so much so that she thought that a little sea was in those eyes. Marvin had the charm which experience brings, the exquisiteness of years lived. But Jaime, on the other hand, had the sheen and the elasticity of stallions and at times it seemed he was flying. However, her mind analysed the abyss which separated the two men.

Marvin returned punctually; sometimes he brought a bottle of apple wine which they drank while they played the game. For Susana, the visits became a part of her Saturday; she awaited them with increasing interest. She observed the details of his clothes and the shoes he wore; each time she saw him as more youthful as if the age difference between him and his son was shortened. She admired his bangs, his smooth skin. She saw him again and again and each time he seemed more distinguished. She remembered when on the rides in his car to the port, he gave them sweets and ice cream. Marvin had asked her what she would do when she grew up; she remembered as if it was yesterday. Mr. Mann hugged her and one evening he gave her a kiss on the forehead. Marvin, such a fine man. What a Marvin, but Marvin, Marvin here, Marvin there. That obsessive idea pushed her to do an impossible but wonderful task because of the difficulty in achieving it. In her insomnia she went distances to have her guardian angel near, Marvin Mann. With her ability she would achieve her goal; she believed in the power of love and with her imagination she created a paradise. It dispelled her fear and as if by magic she found the way to unite her destiny with that of Marvin. She considered it the most convenient option since Jaime was a flirt and changed lovers every Saturday.

On moonlit nights Marvin was her *guitarra*. He travelled in her paper boats; she felt a thrill from dreaming about events that seemed impossible. She imagined and unimagined; she constructed and deconstructed dreams and then, disappointed, threw them to the back of her mind. Two months after the first visit, Mr. Mann learnt through Joelí that his wife had stopped washing because of rheumatism.

Marvin made Carlota understand the advantages of depositing her money in a bank. Then she opened a savings account in the Banco El Porvenir. They all congratulated her because Marvin had made her see reason. He imposed on her the obligation to make fortnightly deposits. Now she cut down on milk because she said that it made her veins bigger, and caused varicose veins; she eliminated red meat, the sacrifice of those poor animals moved her; she did not buy cheese because it aggravated her arthritis; she encouraged her family to eat herbs as Mr. Mann did. When they went to the harbour, she took shrimp already in the *cebiche* since the ones she prepared were better. Everybody at home had a healthy appetite; maybe that's why Susana sang into the wee hours of the morning. What Carlota could not eliminate or reduce were the cocoa and chocolate beverages, since the family was rooted in memories of Africa. Joelí remembered the Garcés family with pride – runaway slaves who were experienced cocoa farmers.

Marvin used the pretext of the game to visit Joelí on Saturdays. One day he gave Carlota a crumpled envelope which he had carried around all week. It was the gift which he gave her for having been the best washerwoman in the world, since the sheets ironed by her had the magic of increasing his desire to embrace Susana. Thus he continued to build a rapport with the family, identifying with the activities of each of its members. It seemed incredible, but chess became a part of that home, that silent atmosphere, interrupted only by Susana's lively *guitarra*. However, he did not see the girl; her parents protected her like a treasure. On her free days, she would attend classes at a beauty school and Marvin congratulated himself on being able to give her parents the impression that he was not interested in the young lady. But one night he deliberately came earlier than usual and when he rang the doorbell, Susana opened the door. It was as if a flash had lit up the darkness, blinded him and made him dumb. Susana, with the charm of youth and the enchantment of spring, stopped being human and became a divine being. His love-struck heart did not stop for ordinary things. He laughed, they both laughed and she planted a kiss on his cheek and ran.

The day I started working in Manolo's beauty salon, so called because its owner is Manuel Enrique Guerra Querine, when I saw that from the walls hung wigs and others adorned the mannequins, I did not understand the reason so I tried to find it in religious principles, superstitions and manias. I thought it was the same way that certain families would hang a sprig of aloe behind the door; Manolo hung wigs with the hope of finding good luck. I counted them: seven hung on the nails, seven rested on a shelf and another seven adorned the mannequins. There was no doubt the owner was superstitious or that that was his special number. The following day I went in search of a numerology book, which explained the value of each letter:

Manuel = 5 + 1 + 7 + 5 + 6 + 4 = 28 = 1
Enrique = 6 + 6 + 2 + 1 + 1 + 5 + 6 = 27 = 9
Guerra = 8 + 5 + 6 + 2 + 2 + 1 = 24 = 6
Querine = 1 + 5 + 6 + 2 + 1 + 6 + 6 = 27 = 9
1 + 9 + 6 + 9 = 25 = 7

I associated him with the seven white horses, seven capital

sins, seven virtues, the seven musical notes, the seven days of the week, the seven colours of the rainbow. Seven was a cabalistic and sacred number used in prayers, as its constant repetition produced certain effects.

Many persons came to Manolo's store, attracted by the quality of the haircuts, the rejuvenation treatment and by the delicate mannerisms of the proprietor. Brought up by his grandmother, he went to great pains to study French and English which gave him a peculiar accent. There was an ambiguity in his gaze and eyes which at times were filled with tenderness. When he spoke for long periods his voice would crack and on realizing it, he would carry a hand to his right brow. He wore a unisex haircut; his hair fell in curls like orange peel.

A young man who came from the country did the cleaning up. Not finding a job anywhere, he accepted Manolo's proposal, good salary and lodging. After doing his chores, he would sit before the mirror to sort the curlers and brushes. He had the profile of a child-god, with blond hair and curly lashes. I did not know whether to call him Mr. or Miss; he looked smilingly at my consternation. Instead of a voice, delicate arpeggios came from his lips. On looking at him a slight tremor invaded me, the fear of seeing him as the exact point where there is fusion of the two sexes into one single image. I had never seen a creature like that before. I felt confused on not finding the exact word to describe him. He examined his profile in the mirror; his languid gaze was that of a woman but when I looked at her/him from the front, his/her face looked serious. I couldn't believe it; he was a man.

He/she handed me the wigs to arrange the hair. As I carried out my task I imagined what the owner would be like. It was then as if she were looking at me, with large brown eyes, delightfully beautiful, because wigs like these, of natural hair, blond, red, honey coloured, would only belong to a person with very fine taste.

I imagined the one I was combing at that moment belonged to

a lady, perhaps called María José, because no other name could fit the owner of such a perfect wig. If it was María José, because beautiful women are called María, maybe like María Felix, and José because that is a name for good luck, of outstanding men like José Martí, José Ingenieros, San José. The owner was not mediocre. Her name could have been taken in memory of José Hernández, the gaucho-poet. I imagined her reciting his verses, an ethereal language, like the breeze which comes from the river; soft, refreshing; she was a dreamer, perhaps a reader of select books. I imagined her clothes; they would be French or bought on Fifth Avenue in Washington or Chicago. She would be an international tourist or an actress of renown, applauded on great stages. Her intimate clothing, her brassiere with medium cups because her breasts would be buds which formed almonds, her vagina a pearl-like shell, marinated in overwhelming juices. I saw her do belly dancing, sliding her bare feet over a marvellous melody, her hips moved to the beat of a salsa. I imagined her to be proudly ambitious, proudly self-centred. On her face shimmered two bright lights with expressions of triumph, wisdom, megalomania and luxury. I felt envious of the applauses and compliments that she would receive. While she twisted between the lights I was absorbed in combing her wig. She had it all; she conquered all. We live in a world where beauty is the magic key to all triumph and is inevitably conditioned to whiteness. To the other wigs I attributed pale faces: white, yellow, matté, with almond eyes, round, oriental-looking red mouths, glamorous, exciting, with old rancour and grotesque pride. Another, with closed eyes and a voice barely audible, told me her story, a vulgar story. Her mother had died when she was a baby. On speaking, she moved her arms and moved her head like a girl who wanted to be a boy. She looked at me with envy as if I were an angel from heaven; her voice exuded hate, anger, vengeance, non-conformity.

During my stay at Manolo's I learnt to respect men, women,

women who looked like men, men who looked like women, ladies who looked like young girls, young girls who looked like mature women, girls who looked like boys and boys who looked like men. There I learnt that each human being has his religion, his faith, his way of praying, his way of kissing and loving and his way of begging. I met Christians who did not practise the doctrine of Christ, others who had taken from God only what suited them; some who said they were Christians but did not love others. When I had a break on the job, I went home and I practised the *guitarra*, even if it was only a piece like a symbolic act, so as not to forget the admirer who continued to send me flowers on Fridays. One afternoon, on leaving work, I was at the point of discovering who that stranger was who sent me flowers since a young man who carried them had stopped to look at a huge fish which two fishermen caught in the river. The animal was so big that even when it was carried on the shoulder the tail dragged on the ground. From then the story in the city was divided: before the *picauro* and after the *picauro*, the name with which they baptized it, since it belonged to a rare species. People gathered to look at it closely and even gaped when they opened it; they saw the intestine, the penis, the gills, but on seeing the testicles, the women drew closer to look at it and surprised, they tried to touch them. On seeing its size, shape, pink colour, velvety texture, more and more women milled around to look closely at the miracle. They all wanted to buy them and in the bustle the owners decided to raffle them but one of them suggested an auction. Whoever paid more would be the owner of the virile organs of such a rare specimen. There was no time; the women fell on the fish's balls to carry away even a little piece. The women hurled questions at the fishermen in an interrogation that seemed unending. One improvised a fishing rod with the hope of catching a similar one, an example which was followed by others.

The shore seemed to be invaded by animated beings. Women,

each time in greater number, remained until midnight with baits in the water and abandoned the place when the tide lowered. Among the curious was the young man who carried the flowers but on seeing Susana close by he ran through the crowd. In the week photos of the porno fish, as some older women called it, appeared and were circulated at their social gatherings. The Minister was forced to comment on it in a two-hour sermon, making the parishioners know that they would be excommunicated if they carried in their bags photographs of the enormous balls. This only encouraged more curiosity and those who did not have the opportunity to see them, bought postcards to verify if, in fact, they were phenomenal. The men did not understand how a stupid fish could triumph in that manner. The men's disgust increased; they took the event as a revelation of the state of desperation in which the women lived, to whom from then on, they endeavoured to give greater pleasure.

The first year of opening the savings account at the Banco El Porvenir my mother, dressed in her Sunday clothes, went as usual to make a deposit; this time she carried the earnings from the sale of the jewellery which Joelí gave to her when she was pregnant. On reaching the corner from the bank, an old man with round lively eyes intercepted her path and told her in a strange accent that he did not know the city or how to read and write but he had won the first prize in the lottery.

After a long conversation on the impossibility of collecting the ticket and Carlota's refusal to buy it from him because she had her money in the bank, they agreed to go there; she withdrew the money while he waited outside.

"Good, please give me what you have, for the love of God."

Carlota received the lottery first prize ticket given to her by the old man and when Joelí and Susana arrived she gave them the news that at last God had remembered them. While she talked she felt sure that she was living a new life but on looking at Joelí's face and hearing him say, "They tricked you," she fainted. When she recovered Susana was by her side; the only thing she could say was that the old man had round eyes; she would recognize him anywhere. Mama came to the conclusion that never again would she put her savings in the bank since nobody would suspect that she had money under the mattress. For some time she kept saying that she would recognize the conman.

Susana had already done the second year of law; she had chosen that career with the intention of defending blacks who were in prison. On taking the classes, it seemed impossible to become a lawyer. During the parties in the faculty, she was the favourite singer. Carlos Zambrano and Cleofé Quiñónez were two companions with whom she returned home. Her passion for Marvin Mann had been drowned under civil and labour codes and international treaties although she continued receiving the bouquets of flowers sent by the mysterious admirer, but it was becoming a routine, so much so that at times the flowers dried up without being seen. Now studying gave her new stimuli; at times her books slept with her. One night she met Ruperto Cañarte; he asked her the time in a strange dialect and that was the reason for starting a long conversation with her during a long walk. When Susana realized what was happening, she was already in the arms of that man, dancing to the rhythm of the bolero in La Dulzura Discotheque, on the port, accompanied by Luz Argentina. There in the semi-darkness, between kisses and hugs, she saw the round, lively eyes of Ruperto. Susana's head began to turn as if the music had unveiled candles on a trip on unknown seas. Her friend, from the table, raised her right thumb several times in celebration of the triumph.

The following day, with laughter and *cebiche*, the two friends celebrated the conquest. For Luz Argentina, Ruperto was an angel fallen from the sky. Look girl, what luck you have. The man is like he was made to order. What looks, what attitude and that way of speaking which is so cute.

Susana laughed and so, day after day, at times missing university, the three enjoyed themselves at the port. It was the period when Susana wore the shortest mini skirts in the city and Ruperto admired the toned shape of her legs. Susana believed that her boyfriend would propose marriage and be the one to take her virginity. He was the first to kiss her lips and he had the virtue of smelling like sun, hot earth, forest and man. Ruperto sang in her ear "La momposina", and taught her dance steps which he had learnt in his country, Calpé. His feet slid from side to side with rhythm and style, forwards and backwards with enviable grace. She was sure that by the end of six months she would be Mrs. Cañarte and she made her parents aware of that possibility. Ruperto is marvelous, he has an expressive gaze, he is an entrepreneur, he has business with important people; yes Mama, he has great economic possibilities. But daughter you shouldn't get too emotional. Yes, I agree with your mother. First you have to analyse it; he could be a liar who is after you only out of an interest in the house. But Papa, how could you even think that Ruperto would have an interest in this old wooden building; I imagine he has houses in his country. You should see him; he's tall, his hair is... it's best that you meet him; you will like him. For Luz Argentina, he's an angel; do you know what an angel is¿ have you seen an angel¿ Well, that is Ruperto.

Susana's parents bought a set of wrought iron chairs that were in style and remodelled the living room. They sent the dining room chairs and the cabinets to be varnished; they lacquered the floor; cleaned the lamps, which had never been touched; they wrote to Matilde and asked her to send the tablecloth and napkins which she was embroidering and to send fresh fruit.

That Sunday, Susana's mother prepared stuffed shells, cassava bread and guava sweets. Now everything shone in the house. Joelí had bought wine and whisky. The doors of the balcony were closed to keep flies from making tracks on the white tablecloth, embroidered by Grandma Matilde. In a porcelain jar, they placed the illusions which the secret admirer sent, and for the first time, Carlota did not lament the robbery of her savings. While Susana bathed with rose-scented soap for good luck, her mother continued to shine the floor as Ruperto would be coming to lunch at midday. Just in case it got hot, Susana wore a blouse with straps and a skirt which ended in pleats. While she got dressed, she hummed "La momposina".

She recognized Luz Argentina from the moment a voice with a ringing accent opened the door of the hall. She brought an apple cake and on seeing the flowers and the sparkling furniture, her laughter filled the air. She was dressed in green lycra which emphasized her buttocks, a little blouse which showed her navel and she wore sandals with high heels. She came with earrings the size of the moon which made her look more like a doll. Susana recognized her perfume, Yves Saint Laurent; she had learnt to distinguish fragrances in Manolo's beauty salon. She had applied it between her breasts, on her navel and between her legs. With her help they gave the final touches to the meal.

Ruperto rang; Carlota went to open the door; on hearing the bell she quickly cleaned her hands on her apron, as at that moment she was applying Old English to the handrail, hid it in one of her dress pockets, and smoothed her hair. Oh, my God! The thief. She closed the door violently and between screams she climbed the steps, spilling the furniture polish as she went. Susana and Luz Argentina took her in their arms, trembling; she could not articulate her words very well. It's him. It's him. It is him. He has round, round eyes. Susana asked her what she was saying since no one could understand her tongue twisting.

Ruperto continued calling now with fear, since he was afraid that they would come back to close the door. Carlota took the sugar and water that Luz Argentina gave her while Susana went to answer the door.

"It's him," whispered Carlota. Ruperto hugged Susana and greeted Luz Argentina with a kiss on her cheek. He carried a bottle of wine and a bouquet of red roses.

Originally from Calpé, he came to Bella Vista because of business. Between the two regions there were good relations and much affluence. From Calpé he had arrived in Bella Vista by sea, a journey which, according to Ruperto, was dangerous because of the currents and sharks. He could have come by plane, which is faster but would not have had the chance to see the beauty of the country which the mangroves offered. He could have come by road; he explained with great detail the problems of customs, the exquisiteness of the Creole meals, the quality of the hotels. Susana went to look for her mother who had recovered from the shock and was reading her Bible and waiting to be introduced to Ruperto Cañarte. She combed Carlota's untidy hair and asked her why she had fainted; her mother answered, "One devil resembles the other."

Ruperto greeted Carlota with a ceremonial bow. During lunch he spoke of different types of crabs; he assured them that he had never tasted stuffed shells like those before. Afterwards he spoke about sole and told a story about why that fish has its mouth twisted. One afternoon the Virgin on strolling by the river asked the sole, what time is it little sole¿ He with a strange, nasal voice said to her, What time is it little sole¿ The Virgin, surprised to see such an ill-mannered fish, said to him, you will remain forever with a twisted mouth. They celebrated the legend with laughter. Afterwards he said that during a crossing of the Mediterranean he had heard the sound of a siren; to everyone it seemed as if Ruperto was a well travelled person. He assured them of the existence of a fish as round as a ball. He spoke of his journey through China, in Shangai, where he ate serpents and spiders. Joelí arrived that moment, shook hands with Ruperto; they opened the bottle of wine and gave a toast to the pleasure of their meeting. While Carlota served apple cake she thought that that man was the one who had robbed her of her savings. It is the same one; he has the round eyes of the old man who surprised me on the corner from the bank. Suddenly Ruperto said, "A Calpense came to Ecuador to buy Beethoven's *Fifth*."

They laughed. Luz Argentina threw her head back and portrayed an attractive arch. Carlota concentrated on her thoughts. He is trying to be funny so that we don't suspect him but it is he, she said to herself.

"A Calpense bought a green car and waited for it to ripen."

"Ha, ha," we laughed in chorus.

The gathering was interrupted by a telephone call for Ruperto. From whom¿ The Minister of Industry¿ Yes. How are you¿ Yes, yes, the contract is already signed. When will the money be ready¿ How much for me¿ Fifty million! Ha, ha, ha. I am having lunch at the home of my future in-laws. Good, brother, we'll see each other. Bye.

Ruperto returned smiling and without any reference to the telephone call resumed his jokes. His voice was that of a triumphant man. He took on the air of a financier and apologized for not being able to stay longer with us, for business reasons. Each time he went to the Garcés, he carried a red rose for Susana, whose imagination was running wild. She also had the right to leave this town, to know other places and Ruperto, who would take her with him, was the most handsome young man in the city. His face showed the mixing of races; his wide forehead, vast intelligence; his hair boasted a strange cut. Although he wasn't a slave to fashion, he dressed elegantly. At times he performed a duet with Susana and sang,

My life is hanging from a rose
because it is beautiful and
although it may have thorns
I am going to take it home.

He would take her out to dance and on spinning her would exclaim: "Hey, girl, this is fantastic. Holy Mary!"

On hot mornings they would go to the port with Luz Argentina. They would have beers then they walked along the beach. They stopped to see the acrobatics of the pelicans and to look at the jetsam full of foam. Sometimes the three ran holding hands betting on which two would first reach the other end of the beach; Ruperto rewarded the winner with a kiss.

In the Garcés house there was the smell of wedding, which seemed to come on the breeze from the river. At nights Ruperto and Susana walked arm in arm; they went to the park and they sat to enjoy the wind that caressed the trees. They took advantage of this time to enjoy themselves and tell each other tidbits.

Pepito asked his teacher, "Miss, is it true that the heart has legs¿"

"No, Pepito."

"Then how is it that every night, upon turning off the light, papa says to my mother: 'Dear heart, open your legs.'"

Susana blushed but did not dare stop him. She did not want anything to separate her from Ruperto. After that, without any apprehension, he told her funny stories with colourful vocabulary and gesticulation. On hearing the jokes, her lips curled sensuously and her nostrils flared; each word increased the pleasure flowing through her skin.

"Holy Mary," he laughed.

Meanwhile Marvin would watch from his terrace, through his binoculars, Susana's love scenes with that stranger. For him everything was lost; she was practising her charms on the stranger. Who could have introduced her to that man¿ Where had he come from¿ He would make sure that that impertinent person would not ruin Susana's life or his. A thousand suspicions tormented him; insomnia was making him weary; he felt incapable of defending his love. Sometimes he felt too old to try for her, but overcome with desire, he erased the barriers of years, colour and class. So, while he watched his little rabbit losing herself in Ruperto's caresses, he became filled with desperation.

He felt tired, as if he was suddenly hit by old age. Stumbling, he went to his room but that night he found the solution to his bitterness: he would take Susana to work next to him in the bank; she would be his private secretary.

One Saturday when they were playing chess, he told Joelí that it was time for Susana to stop working in the beauty salon; it was necessary for her to practise what she was learning at the university. The father accepted the suggestion but he spoke of the difficulty in obtaining work where they would give her permission to study.

After fifteen days Margarita Mann, motivated by curiosity to know the young man who was visiting Susana in a new red Ford car, went to the Garcés house on the pretext of delivering a cheque which Ruth Mann had sent as thanks for services rendered. It was her opportunity to introduce herself to Ruperto. The two reminisced on adventures on stilts and rafts in the winter, when the streets became rivers. When Ruperto discovered that Margarita worked in a bank, he suggested that she take Susana to work in that institution.

"I will speak to my father. I don't know if they accept negroes."

Skin colour played a role of great importance in the life of the country, the city and families. It was the standard which made white shine and those who pretended to be white. It was an Aladdin's lamp with which they worked miracles. The country's honour and history were secondary to white colour, the emblem of nobility and hierarchy. After serving herself a glass of wine, Margarita said goodbye to Susana with a kiss.

In the middle of September, the wigs came back into my hands; Manolo demanded detail in the finish of the hairstyles since the owners would be attending a high society party. He insisted on punctuality and care. He would provide lunch so as not to waste time. He cancelled all requests for time off and postponed holidays. The telephone was ringing constantly and on answering, at the other end of the line were sweet voices, pretentious with refinement. They were calling to recommend that I show my professional ability in the style of this and that wig because the owners' engagements were of exceptional importance.

Manolo's shop drew women overcome by sadness, with new wrinkles, worries, problems, with signs of grey and tiredness. Manolo listened patiently to their problems and with understanding eyes he would contemplate death disguised as old age. He would be responsible for reviving these dried roses with tenderness and shine on their petals. His job involved removing the shadowy aspect which they carried to give them what they wanted – youthful airs. On those sad flowers he read their frustrations, their concerns, their anxieties because the face is a page on which we write our story, our desires, our victories and our failures. Manolo hid the ravages of time, the vengeance of God. With slow hand movements the comedy began and finally the client would thank him on seeing their honey, lilac, red, black, blond hair with shining eyes, smooth skin, provocative lips. It was his triumph, he had reconstructed the flower even though the perfume was fleeting.

Fifteen days before the party Manolo went on a diet of grapes and apples since he was one pound overweight. He would arrive at the shop an hour after his usual time, as suddenly he was doing exercise classes, going to the Sauna and having Turkish baths. At that time it was considered wise not to sunbathe; he applied a mask, specially made for him, of sea turtle oil carried from the Galápagos Islands. He increased his habit of looking at himself in the mirror and combing his hair.

Men with leather shoes and European haircuts came to the salon, as well as businessmen with executive briefcases. Singers, lawyers, doctors, priests from the city, others came from abroad specially invited.

Manolo on hearing that I would be leaving his employ in a few days since Marvin Mann told papa that I should come to the bank, invited me to the party, which took place on the day of Mercedes, which everyone spoke so much about. I went with Luz Argentina; Ruperto could not accompany me because of business; his friend, the Minister, asked him to come see him.

Manolo placed us at the front of the stage, excused himself and left. Those present wore lamé, silk and brocade outfits. A singer named María Soledad opened the show rendering a ballad. Next entered a blonde *salsa* dancer, with bare breasts and a g-string bikini, shaking her hips. The audience stood and applauded her.

Next the candidates were introduced to the judges. They walked slowly down the runway in long, tight dresses, with plunging necklines. The mistress of ceremonies read the profile of the aspirants to the panel, which had one common denominator, they had lived in Paris. She read the name of the winner. The public applauded. The slimmest candidate had won the crown; she accepted the sash amidst applause, tears and kisses. We approached her to congratulate her. Shocked, we recognized Manolo who was viewing the whole event with sad joy.

Believing that the personnel manager of the Banco El Porvenir on seeing my application would observe me closely, I practised steps and greetings beforehand. I wondered whether I should extend my hand or wait to be told to sit. The next problem was the dress; would it be appropriate to wear a miniskirt or go with a tailored style in linen and a light colour¿ I took down dresses, skirts, pants, blouses but on seeing myself in the mirror I didn't think they were appropriate. Finally I selected a pleated skirt and silk blouse with long sleeves.

Margarita was in the office. On seeing me she objected to my simplicity. Ready to show off her experience, she took me to the bathroom with her. She redid my make-up and shook a little flask; she applied perfume to my earlobes. "You are ready," she muttered. As if by a miracle, with that fragrance my fear disappeared. She introduced me to the personnel manager; he looked up.

"But she is black."

He went immediately to speak to the manager. Marvin calmed him.

"In God's vineyard, there are all types."

When the personnel manager returned, he told me that I was accepted. An employee was made responsible for showing me what to do. I went to the window to be a cashier. After one week I was wearing the uniform of the institution.

The clientele was shocked to see me.

"Have you seen a black woman at my window¿"

"This is the limit! Tomorrow I'm withdrawing my money from the bank."

Before a month had passed the director of the section had received eleven complaints. The spokesperson passed on the complaints to the Manager, but Marvin was prepared for the counter attack. His determination to have her near him was not a matter of reason but the heart. He would not give up his efforts to have her as his secretary – his only objective which, as a major shareholder of the bank, he was sure to achieve before anyone else could become her boss. Now he was leaving his office and without reason he went to see the torment of his life. Reanimated, he returned to his office to continue thinking about his change of secretary. He was sure that Susana had entered his world; his anxieties overflowed making him forget his age and position. His love was a flame that had become a furnace which kept him tormented.

At every opportunity Ruperto asked Susana how the bank worked and the amount of money she handled; she talked like a spinster to her cat. He rewarded her with kisses all over like a bird that pecked over and over at some fruit. Once, by those threads of memory, he remembered his mother and on remembering her he felt the kicks she gave him in his head when she discovered that he had wet the bed. The thought that he hated her as much as his drunken father drove him mad.

"You wet yourself again."

Over the years that memory left a lasting impression on his infancy. He assured her that his parents were an odd pair but soon he would fill the conversation with jokes so that Susana would not perceive his tragedy, convinced that he was conceived without love. Until that moment, he had a plan wavering between fiction and reality, in which Susana would play a central role, because from the time he met her he thought that she was the ideal woman for his project, although he never believed she would be the daughter of the woman he had conned. To choose a young black woman, a university student and a lover of music, he believed was the most intelligent decision of his life. He smelt her purse; it smelt of money; he waited for the opportunity to hug her, call her my love, my little queen, my dear heart, my Susanita. Then with a very heavy voice he told her that the transfer which he expected had not arrived and he needed to settle his hotel bills. He kissed her hands. She was moved. But Ruperto, why didn't you tell me this before? That's why we are engaged. Don't worry, tell me in confidence when you need money. He rewarded her with a kiss on her mouth. She handed him the envelope with her salary from the bank.

"I'll give it back to you, my love."

But he took to asking her for money and she was happy to know that she was alleviating her boyfriend's situation; that, between flattery and words of gratitude, he told her in her ears how much he loved her.

"It's only a loan, dear."

"Don't worry, Ruperto, it is so small."

The moon appeared from beneath the hills, a whistle came to us from the gate, it was Luz Argentina, she cameup.

"Hello, I'm hungry," she laughed.

The two of us laughed also on seeing her arrive with her hair in tangles, and wearing a long gown whose transparency revealed her nipples. For one moment, Ruperto's gaze rested on those buds, then he looked at me and we laughed. I offered her two oranges and while Ruperto peeled them, she complained because they had not left supper for her at home; a friend of her stepfather's had come and they gave her the meal. She criticized those people who choose certain strategic times to visit. Luz Argentina laughed and laughed and every time she laughed, her breasts would jump up and down. In desperation, she sucked an orange as the juice flowed at times down the corners of her mouth; she caught it with the tip of her fingers. She continued sucking the fruit with exciting groans while Ruperto and I continued observing her. She picked up the other orange and took it to her lips; it seemed that her appetite was huge. On finishing it, she took off the skin and devoured the pulps which still had juice. She sat back in the armchair and closed her eyes. She seemed tired, smiling; from the bottom of her dream smiles flowered. I did not want to wake her for fear of stirring up her appetite. At times when some sand fly bothered her she moved her thighs to frighten it. How long she remained like that, I don't know, maybe until almost midnight. She continued dreaming, maybe about some pleasant sin, because she was smiling. I woke her up so she could go home. I looked out of the window. I wanted to see her enter her house but I could not; the darkness protected her. I didn't hear her but her voice continued to resonate like something permanent, like the things which go but remain next to one. Almost immediately Ruperto said goodbye.

When he arrived at the hotel, a fixed idea kept him going; he recognized that the risk was high; he was aware of it. He considered the danger natural, but he could not allow any more delays; everything had marinated for several weeks and he had analysed it in detail in his sleepless nights.

Still the plan made him nervous; when he thought about it, a kind of electric current ran through his body. He tossed and turned in bed as he put the final touches to his plan. Drawn by the plan, he felt an obsession with risk. It was now impossible for him to forget it, the pleasure of once again going on an adventure which would bring into play his vigour and his talent. He walked along the hotel piazza until it was time to visit Susana; he tried to serenade her.

At the Garcés house he spoke about Calpé and a bank employee who was now a millionaire; he sighed:

"My love, you could also take a note from each drawer."

"Impossible, I am not a thief."

Ruperto reacted passionately. He kissed her several times. He was more charming than ever. He asked her to hum "La Momposina". She went for the *guitarra* and they sang with the accompaniment of the instrument. Then he invited her to dance in the living room. While he embraced her he whispered in her ears,

"Promise me to take one note tomorrow."

"No, don't insist."

The following day Susana handed him the removed note. He lifted her up; now she seemed more adorable to him; she had obeyed him. The following week when Ruperto arrived at the Garcés house, he carried a new repertoire of stories and he unleashed his good humour. As soon as Susana stopped laughing he told her other stories; the only action of the young girl was to hide her excitement. Ruperto laughed not because of what he was telling her but because of the satisfaction of having liberated her from unnecessary modesty.

One afternoon he appeared with a more important plan. He was not there to receive little dribblings of one or two notes taken three times per week by Susana. He spoke to her clearly; she needed to give him proof of her love. They would marry and leave for his country where eternal happiness awaited them but she would have to cooperate or else there would be no marriage. She snuggled closer to him, smelt his cologne, breathing deeply.

Ruperto's shirt was a designer brand. How he fascinated her. He took advantage of that admiration to tell her his plan: they would rob the bank.

At first for Susana it was madness, an impossibility, but after a short time she accepted the project. She was afraid of losing him and began to provide him with information about the operations of the windows to the large register, the vault, the guards, the alarms. Ruperto rewarded the information with caresses. She saw him as a wizard, a demon or an angel. She did not understand the impulses which converged in danger.

Susana trembled at the thought of failure and her imprisonment. The plan made her nervous and in her office they noticed how prone she was to shouting for whatever reason. The lemon infusion given to her by Carlota did not serve any purpose. The date of the robbery drew near; only fifteen days were left and in her insomnia, she tried to put her thoughts in order; she examined, one by one, the steps she should take on the appointed day. She began to lose weight and her appetite. Mentally, she studied the position of each of the guards, the possible reaction of her colleagues and above all, the internal alarm circuit which she studied every day; she contemplated the deactivation of this control mechanism.

Her cash register should have the maximum amount of money. Ruperto would approach her window disguised as an old man, with a stick and hat which would cover most of his face. He would be wearing a big moustache with spots on each cheek. On the fifteenth of December at one in the afternoon he would approach the window; he would threaten Susana with a gun; she, without saying a single word and without setting off the alarm, would hand him all the money. When Ruperto was outside of the bank, she would pretend to faint. Susana breathed as if she were out of breath; she needed to repeat the scene as it would take place and in the practice she got taken up with the dream of being with her lover. Sometimes, at home she would get up in search of a glass of water; the silence of the dawn filled her with longings for the smell of shellfish which came from the river. She grabbed the *guitarra* and pulled it towards her chest as if it were Ruperto. But as the day got closer, she could not avoid the fear which was growing inside of her, the fear of obtaining so much happiness with that young man who had fallen from the sky. After the robbery he would remain hidden in the hotel pretending to be paying bills and answering letters that had supposedly arrived. He would write in the morning and leave hurriedly to mail them. In the hotel, he had kept his old man's disguise hidden in a double bottomed suitcase and which he now took out to practise the behaviour and limp of an old man.

Carlota approached the couple as they were reviewing the plan but, tired of speaking without being listened to, she went to sit under the ticking clock. She nodded, her eyes half closed out of fear that they were up to something. Determined to protect her daughter's honour, she pretended to be sleeping. The years had taught her that experience was what really counts. Moreover, she could not get out of her mind Ruperto's resemblance to the trickster who had stolen her savings, but she doubted that it was he.

Susana got up to get two glasses of wine at that moment. Carlota, spying from where she was seated, realized that they were planning something serious judging from the looks of the couple.

In the following days, although she noticed that Susana was as skittish as a nervous goat, she took refuge in prayer, in the hope that it would keep the devil away from her daughter's soul. Susana had started rising late and she had no time to do her exercises but stayed in bed, stretching and bending her legs, and moving her body from side to side, her thoughts firmly fixed on the bank robbery. No matter what position she was in, what time it was or where she was, she was confronted by it. She began talking to herself and falling asleep on her feet. One night she dreamt of the prince who woke up the Sleeping Beauty after so many years of sleeping; on another, a world where there was neither night nor day, nor death.

On yet another occasion, she thought she was on a crag looking at a wide plain totally painted in green and she saw trees which looked like people, or people who looked like trees, people walking barefoot on the grass and as they walked seeds sprung up and turned into trees. Later, she thought that she was in jail, in a cold, dark cell and as she woke up, she felt dizzy. The idea of the robbery seemed to be a joke, one that would take her into Ruperto's arms. She would travel to other countries, own property and jewellery.

She made her way to the bank, preoccupied with the thought that the plan might fail and she tried to smile with the clients while Marvin suffered in silence. It was difficult for her to make the slightest movement without being seen and it was for this reason that Marvin knew as much about her as she knew about herself. Now, he wanted her more although he realized the error of having put her in his way. He thought of hiring her as a secretary so she would earn a higher salary. She would be his confidante but he thought that his daughter Margarita would detect his longings, since Susana's physical attributes were like some sort of magnet to him. He put the idea out of his mind and checked the documents.

As the day of the robbery drew nearer, Susana constantly remembered her mother's face; she saw her counting the rosary beads when she was ill; her mother would check her pulse and listen closely to her chest to see if she was getting better. But when she spoke to Ruperto and felt his caresses, Carlota's face faded. Then she promised him to have the nerves of steel during the robbery. They would enjoy their honeymoon in Venice, sail on the gondolas, visit Paris, touch the ironwork of the Eiffel Tower, go to London. They would work in some city in Europe. Ruperto had assured her that it would be easy to find a job; they would love each other for the rest of their lives; they would have children.

The day before the robbery Susana went over the plan; her pulse raced, so nervous was she that she lost her balance and fell flat on her face. Ruperto was afraid that she would have an accident or back out since when he kissed her lips he realized that she was trembling.

At a quarter past twelve Susana went to the cashier's desk for more money and returned to her counter window with a full pouch which she would hand over to Ruperto. Discreetly she took her handkerchief and wiped away the drops of sweat that were running down her forehead. She nervously counted the bills; her hands trembled; she felt more afraid than she was minutes before. Marvin, who was watching her on his television screen, was amazed by Susana's state; something was happening to her; her whole body was shaking as if she were suffering from a sudden bout of malaria. Her beauty, her gracefulness and her charm had abandoned her; now she was sweating more profusely and constantly looking at the entrance.

"Guardian angel, do not desert me now," she implored.

Immediately Marvin called the personnel manager and instructed him to replace Susana with another cashier. Ruperto, disguised as an old man and carrying a big bag under his arm, was second in line in front of her counter and she felt her stomach cramp and the undeniable desire to go to the bathroom. She ran; she didn't manage to pull down her underwear and defecated, soiling everything in her path. Marvin and his secretary closed the counter and asked the doctor to examine her. He gave her a prescription and ordered her to rest for the remainder of the day.

When she looked at herself in the mirror she could see the distress caused by the unsuccessful robbery. She realized that it was not as easy as Ruperto had assured her. He returned to the hotel without the disguise having changed in a hallway and stashed it in his bag.

He preferred to talk about other matters apart from the robbery so as not to frighten Susana anymore. He sang "La Momposina", but once more memories of his childhood surfaced in his mind so that soon he spoke of the blows he had received from his mother when he wet his bed. Susana agreed to carry out the robbery the following Monday. She kissed him on the lips and asked him to forgive her but that the robbery would take place on Monday. He smiled and returning the caress said to her, "Don't worry, love, these things happen."

Susana took the *guitarra* and tried to pluck a *bolero* but she couldn't. Her fingers trembled; her nervousness made worse by the postponement of the robbery. She sighed. Carlota, who heard her, sensed that something unusual was happening. Her daughter was going through a difficult period for her sweat was strong. She went for two glasses of juice and sandwiches. Her daughter thanked her. She noticed her bad breath as she went near to her. Susana invited her to sit. She searched Ruperto's eyes and was sure that it was he who had stolen her savings. Her doubts disappeared; her daughter's fiancé looked very much like the robber, but she would keep her secret. Since Ruperto showed no signs of nervousness, the mother started to doubt again; she said to herself: I am wrong; he is a gentleman and a friend of the Minister. He is not the one who robbed me. Dear God, forgive me! She admitted her mistake at last and even found her future son-in-law to be pleasant.

They looked at the sky, across which grey clouds were now spreading. A foul wind was enveloping the people, the animals and the hilltops; it was the oil refinery giving off toxic smells. To Carlota it seemed like a long arm crushing everything in its path. It brought back to her memories of her sky in Plenilunio – the sky of her youth, blue, resplendent in August, a sky which looked like the sea turned upside-down.

"Why do we always go around looking for trouble in life¿" Carlota asked them as she went out. They did not answer. So forceful was the question that Susana looked into her mother's eyes. Her daughter was the only one she would have in her old age. The thought caused Susana to hesitate. She leaned on her fiance's shoulder and cried. Ruperto told her it was better this way. Crying would ease the tension. He stroked her back. Susana was living a nightmare. She felt strange, listless, unable to get up. She felt better after crying; filled with renewed courage, enough to tell Ruperto that she could not face another risk.

"Then you will not live to the fullest," he told her. To distract her and get her to change her mind, he talked to her about a salt mine in Zipaquirá, near Bogotá, a place in the mountain with streets and avenues lit by special lights which led to a temple. Then he spoke of the procession of the chair bearers, numerous competitors who carried on their backs chairs filled with the flowers of the region – a colourful spectacle which he so longed to take her to see.

But now Susana could envision nothing else but prison for Ruperto. Her silence meant that the plan would not be carried out. She was a black woman; weak, unable to make decisions; of what use would she be to him? He needed a strong partner with nerves of steel, because he had big plans in mind, plans which required bravery. Susana kissed his hands submissively but at that moment he considered leaving her. She really would not serve his purpose; she didn't know how to enjoy the thrill of danger. He wanted a brave woman, daring, greedy for money, with a different mentality. Ruperto hid his anger and hatred, for the Garcés girl was a cowardly black-woman, a nobody. She understood her fiance's disgust but feigned tenderness. What would she be without him? She so loved his caresses and his voice!

His long silence served to convince her. She saw Ruperto as a giant.

"Okay, next Monday we'll carry out the plan as agreed," she

promised him.

He took her in his arms and kissing her, said, "If we pull this off, I will know once and for all that you love me."

The wind brought with it a pleasant smell which I thought came from the flowers of my secret admirer, but I noticed that it was a different smell. Its perfume made you forget everything and think only about the person wearing it. On the verandah, its wall bordering Luz Argentina's house, we sat leafing through a magazine. We read the titles and stopped to comment on things we considered to be of interest. Sometimes we laughed with reason and sometimes for no reason at all.

Ruperto strolled along the verandah, puffing out his chest, content at breathing in the perfumed air. The wind brought more and more of the aroma as though it wanted to monopolize the atmosphere. Although I lacked an acute sense of smell, I noticed that it filled the air with voluptuousness. We continued reading, needing to steer my mind away from the subject of the robbery, but that fragrance hovered around like a serpent. Ruperto opened his arms and breathed in more deeply as if he wanted to absorb all the perfume himself. I tried to smile and talked of everything and nothing in an effort to entertain him, but he was lost in himself and turned the pages without saying a single word. I understood that he was intoxicated with the smell coming from the neighbour's house, a smell which invaded his body through every pore. I began to feel embarrassed, disgusted by that exciting, erotic aroma. I wondered, experiencing several degrees of anger, where the hell that damned but pleasant odour was coming from and bit by bit I was giving it a name. I concluded that the strong aroma came from the breathing of a naked, beautiful woman with a unique laugh, a temptation coming from a known person. Ruperto's eyes reflected an unusual charm; he looked at the magazine and jubilant smiles played around his lips. Confused, I began to sing.

My life is tied to a rose because it's beautiful...

But I noticed that his thoughts were wandering in the surge of the fragrances; that perfume brought with it the essence of a strange woman, seductive, worrying, overpowering. A dark rage began to fill me. Ruperto's face vibrated with pleasure for the gentle breeze disturbed him profoundly. He turned the leaves of the magazine with nervous fingers. I viciously cursed the sin that transported that perfume, steeped in fresh orange blossoms, to which had been added Affection, Forget-me-not, Follow me Follow me, Water of seven chakras, Love Flower, Humming bird heart and an ounce of gold.

That fragrance carried the scent of a luscious body, made from the essence, sweat, dreams and longings of that continent. I understood it; it was a threat to me. But who could that cursed vessel be? Ruperto stopped suddenly; he was obviously bound up by that aroma. It was as if he had seen the image next door; he wet his lips as if he was savouring it. I got the impression that he intended to fly towards the source of the perfume; I imagined him, like a spider, crawling up the wall that separated my house from my neighbour's. I looked at the cord where Luz Argentina had her clothes drying, her panties, bras, her slips. It was from there that the perfume was reaching us. Now I was drowning in the world created by those waves of smells. I was the one who had turned my friend's clothing into delicious odors. It was I, and not Ruperto, who had given a physical shape to the perfume; I who had fashioned a disorganized scandal of assumptions because of the essences reaching my house. Night came, dragging along a perfumed wind originating from my neighbour's underwear. He saw the great worry in my eyes. I thought that she had done it purposely to excite Ruperto's senses.

"Good, you've finally decided," he said.

He looked at me from head to toe, trying to hide his anger. He said that the entire plan was easy; in a matter of minutes we would be millionaires. Moreover, old Marvin Mann will not suspect that you are involved in the robbery; he is such a close friend of your Dad. I felt reassured; I ended up believing that he was right. I didn't want to lose him. I still had time to overcome my weaknesses; we would strike on the appointed day. He stopped to kiss me. This is the way I like you; you are adorable this way. He lowered his mouth to my breasts; I felt the world rock.

It was two days before the robbery; Ruperto detected the cowardly nature of the young girl as she responded evasively to his questions. Joelí went to open the door to the hallway where someone was knocking at that moment. Marvin Mann appeared; he had come to play chess and to find out how Susana was feeling after her illness days ago. It was a surprise to Joelí for he had not heard about what had happened. He attributed it to the change in food; that day he had brought saltpetre to serve her with baked plantains. Marvin was introduced to Ruperto. He had imagined him to be a superman seeing that he had stolen the love of his rabbit, but he thought that he was a trickster and bad luck to Susana for having found a man who wore coffee-coloured shoes with black pants. While they moved the pieces, Marvin watched the young girl; she was his desire which he had to put aside. At times he thought it was better this way because he was growing increasingly anxious and he was a married man with two children. As the game continued, tears of pain and rage coursed within him. Susana laughed with Ruperto. She was wearing a strapless blouse which left her shoulders exposed. Marvin followed her movement through the mirror. He lost every game.

"Marvin, you have your head in the clouds," Joelí told him.

That Sunday Luz Argentina came over; she had been invited to lunch. She came dressed enticingly, wearing a flower in her hair. She wore bracelets, necklaces and rings on all her fingers. She burst in laughing, carrying a packet of fish to teach us a recipe she had recently learnt; her eyelashes shone with mascara. I wanted to shout at her: "Enough with conspiring with the wind to send your perfume to Ruperto! Enough with spying on us to blow your scents in our faces!" I wanted to tell her what Jesus said to his disciples, 'One of you will betray me.'

I felt like telling her about Napoleon when he came face to face with Fouché: "You would do better to bury this dagger." But my friend, ingenuously amusing, laughed and sent me an ambiguous glance. I backed down. Was I the one with crazy thoughts in my head? It was scary living besieged with suspicions, living in misery, for in the silence of the early morning the laughter played havoc with my sleep! Now she unleashed all her charms and it seemed to me that she was boldly pretending to be naïve.

Luz Argentina greeted me with a kiss on the cheek.

"Darling," she said.

I felt relieved because these formalities were a part of our friendship. I was wrong. Why would I believe that she would be disloyal to me? If she always came to the house to chat, to go walking, so many years of building a close friendship with childish games and confidences, how stupid could I be? In the kitchen she burst out laughing, opened her arms and exclaimed: "A stove with an oven; this sounds like a wedding to me!" Now it was my turn to burst out laughing. "Yes and soon. What do you think?" She froze, her body stiff, her words suspended. I remembered when we both used to run around the yard playing statues; she would shout to me: "Statue!" and I would stop, hardly breathing, hardly blinking.

She stood there in the middle of the kitchen, absorbed. Then she started to clean the fish with salt and lime, moving around quietly as though she were in darkness unable to think and someone had covered her mouth. She sighed the sigh of a sick person at whose door death was knocking but her blackout was short-lived; she came back to life and hummed Ruperto's favourite song, the one he usually sang with me when he was happy. Now she was softly singing our song, "La Momposina". Why that tune precisely? And she laughed as she sang,

My life is tied to a rose
Because it is beautiful and even though it has thorns...
Ay, Praise Mary!

"Damn it, damn her a thousand times!" Why should she be singing our song¿ Why blessed Changó, was she finishing the song with the same exclamation¿ My heart now beat as if it were on a tightrope, waiting. She, my soul mate, singing exactly the same part in the same way and with the same strange accent. I looked at her out of the corner of my eye; but "what cheek!" And, as if ants were walking all over me, I began to scratch my head. I thought that it was dangerous to keep her friendship, that friendship we had had for so many years. The song stoked my jealousy. I felt as if I was choking, as if I were shut up in a sealed room. She, singing "La Momposina", exclaiming. "Ay, Praise Mary!" in the same way as Ruperto. Why didn't she sing something current, a *meneíto*, a *merengue*¿ She continued singing, looking at me furtively, somewhat mischievously. She stood up on tiptoes to look for the condiments in the pantry; to me her wish to torment me was obvious, having exposed her betrayal. She sprinkled more salt on the fish.

Suddenly, "Hey! That reminds me of the salt mines in Zipaquirá!" she exclaimed.

"You know something about them¿"

"Yes."

I had no doubt she and Ruperto were deceiving me. I was sure of their betrayal. Anxious to stop her I told her of my relationship with Ruperto, who adored me. He had promised me eternal love. He was going to take me to discover his country. She stopped looking at the dish she was preparing, her black eyes flashed. Disconcerted, her lips traced a half-mocking smile and she began to talk again, telling a joke.

Pepito asked his teacher: "Miss, is it true that the heart has legs...¿" I didn't listen to her. My head was spinning; I heard her breathe; her breathing bothered me. She moved her legs, her buttocks made little movements like a cat in heat.

I looked at her closely; she wore a designer blue jeans. Where did she get money to buy such fine pants¿ Who could have given it to her¿ I asked myself. I admitted that the new pants had something to do with my boyfriend. I had known her for such a long time, I knew her economic situation inside out. Now she had learned to pretend in the tug-of-war over Ruperto. I remembered our lives as little girls when we really loved and cared mutually for each other. The feeling of sharing with her the man I loved filled me with resentment. The make-up made her seem more attractive and I regretted showing it to her. After an internal struggle, while she was mixing the stew I asked her what was the brand of her jeans.

She looked at me with the flutterings of one who is jealous and choosing her words she said, "From Calpé."

Her response to me was like a bolt of lightning. It wasn't that I was looking for hidden meanings in words but this woman was on the verge of driving me crazy. Apart from the unease she caused in my thoughts, she was trying to take away my dignity. I remembered the perfume of her underwear and the transformation in Ruperto.

Papa entered the kitchen with three bottles of beer to go with the cocoa. She said smiling, "No, don Joelí, I am not preparing cocoa; I am practising a recipe from Calpé."

Panic ran from my head to my feet; something in me vibrated in circles, I forgot that I had to prepare the avocado salad with lettuce. I made a mistake; instead of putting salt into the soup, I added sugar. My friend's words, her slenderness, her laughter, her earrings, her perfume, for the first time filled me with envy and I knew what it was to hate. Luz Argentina had taken off her mask; she enjoyed hurting me; it was only left for her to say that she and Ruperto were lovers. I should do something, but what¿ My head was spinning; ideas came and went in waves. I was walking as if I was drunk, suspended in the air. I must have been pale because papa asked me what was happening to me. She smiled and without need, walked around swaying her bottom. Then she cut up parsley on the board; she handled the knife as if she were cutting somebody: it was a quick, violent sound; her pleasure in the cuts was obvious. I felt as if she were cutting me up into bits.

I went to the kitchen sink then I uncovered the pots, picked up the cloth to clean off the table and moved the pots again. On picking up a cup, it fell and broke into pieces.

Ruperto arrived after midday. As usual, he kissed both of us on the cheek. He greeted my parents with a solemn nod and then shook their hands. He exchanged glances with my friend; she smiled and made a sensual gesture. There was no doubt they wanted each other. I placed Luz Argentina beside Ruperto. I sat in front of them to scrutinize their eyes but they were enjoying the pleasure of being together. It seemed to me that placing her so close to him was the best idea I had ever had in my life. I didn't know what to talk about; I was sorry that I had invited her. She took out her handkerchief; with gentle movements she fanned herself, spreading her fragrance. In my mind, I saw Ruperto as a candy stuck to her body. She continued to pretend being hot just so he would smell her perfume. How brazen! Go to hell! Me playing the part of the useful idiot and them happily enjoying a meal here in my house¿ He took the opportunity to tell us that the Minister, his personal friend, had written to him and showed us a paper with a signature. Luz Argentina leaned closer to him, exposing her breasts and with a polished voice she asked him to get her a job.

I watched her throughout the entire lunch; I did not miss one single movement. Her eyes shone with delight and she continued smiling. Now she adjusts her neckline; she looks for ways to provoke him as if she were saying: "Look what beautiful breasts I have." Slut, coming without a bra so that Ruperto could admire her breasts!

Mama brought the glasses and papa filled them with beer. My friend raised her glass, looked me up and down and said: "To your health, Susana."

The sea lay stretched out at the feet of the city and nipped it from time to time. On that day, it submerged its joy in its unfathomable depths. I was walking with Ruperto on the beach. I banished all my doubts. He loved me. He said so for the umpteenth time and that he had no intention whatsoever of falling in love with Luz Argentina. My silly ideas and my jealousy made him smile as he thought they were absurd. I now felt that my attitude was ridiculous – to have cried, imagined betrayal. It was love that made me distrustful. We had come to the harbour to finalize the details of the agreement. He made an effort to conceal his fears about my reservations as there was less than a day left and he had to be sure about my role. With a twig, he sketched in the sand the entrance to the bank. He would walk, leaning on the walking stick; he would use make-up, which he had prepared so that he would look wrinkled. He would wear a hat and keep the money in his briefcase so that the guards wouldn't be suspicious. He would be like any client withdrawing funds. He rehearsed step by step until he reached an imaginary line, which he drew in the sand. When he was at my window he would take out a pistol wrapped in a handkerchief so that only Susana would see it. He would say softly, "This is a hold-up." When he reached the exit I would faint. He would get into his car, which he would have left with the motor running. He would park elsewhere, dispose of his disguise and take another car to the hotel. Later, he would collect his car.

He made me practise how I would hand him the bags with the money he had requested previously; quickly and calmly so that not even one bill would fall. I looked at the sea. It was a huge blue cardboard. Birds were flying hurriedly south; there was not the slightest ripple of a breeze; the canoes and fishermen's boats lay motionless. There were no bathers in the water or on the beach. The sun, imprisoned in the clouds, protested with a sliver of sunlight. I saw a palm tree with birds that made strange sounds. At times they raised their heads and then hid them again under their wings. In the distance the dogs barked, frightened. The place became dark and the air was still. Ruperto suggested that I should get up early and take a very cold bath and a cup of sweetened water with ten drops of valerian. While I listened to him I absorbed the sadness of the sea and suddenly I said to him, "I will not involve myself in that robbery." He slapped me and screamed, "You are a coward, damn you!" I ran towards the road but he came after me. He held me by force and he was trembling. "Forgive me." He didn't let go of my waist but insisted that I forgive him. Faced with this harassment I mumbled, "It's OK, we'll do it; I swear."

My parents had the lights on and they welcomed us, worried because morning seemed to be turning back to night. They had received a letter from doña Ofelia Seminario, widow of Pino. She told them that she was confined to a home for the aged and she was spending her last days there. They had already decided that they would bring her to live with us. Mama interrupted the conversation and when she became aware of my smell, she opened her eyes wide. I had a strange smell. She stopped in front of Ruperto and her eyes immediately filled with tears. She tried to speak as everything began to fall. "Earthquake! earthquake!" the alarm was unanimous.

We ran into the street. Ruperto disappeared in the crowd. People were on their knees screaming. Houses hit against each other; light posts fell; sirens and ambulances wailed; streets opened and the river roared. In a few minutes the face of the city was transformed into a crossroads of weeping that echoed in the air.

"My God, save us. Blessed St. Barbara, have pity on us!"

We returned home and picked up the pieces of glass that were scattered on the floor and under the furniture. We tried to put things in order but another tremor shook the house. The plates fell; the glass from the cabinet fell and shattered. A more powerful chorus of prayers was offered. Mama went for her discoloured, soiled print of Jesus the Great Power and put it in her bosom. She tried to blackmail Him, offering Him three rosaries every night. She would give better meals to the madwoman in the district if He spared us. We ran to the park which was now a sea of prayer, weeping and terror; the Cathedral was full of parishioners and the faithful were kneeling in the street.

Never before had the sea swelled as it did now. Waves of up to four meters demolished everything in their path. Jumping over ditches and poles, I reached Cleofé and asked him if he had seen Ruperto. His reply was no. I looked for him everywhere. I questioned the neighbours but they hadn't seen him. The earth trembled again. The houses sounded like crates of empty bottles. The people were running through the streets clutching their children on their shoulders. Some of the townsfolk fell, some because of the tremor, some because of their terror; others thought the end of the world was coming and consumed great quantities of alcohol. Roars coming from the sea, now a lion, created greater confusion.

People left the church; the priest took out the Virgin on a portable platform and placed her in the centre of the park. The church bells ringing on their own increased the alarm. The multitude crowded around the sacred images. The people from the hills came down like an avalanche. The adults began to confess their sins. They came out, amidst shouts each one louder than the other – deprecations, slander which caused imprisonment, blotches on the honour of ladies, embezzlement; personal enrichment by mayors, administrators, councillors, board members, directors, governors, deputies; infidelity, incest, promises to recognize disowned children, explanations from mothers who had given incorrect surnames to their children, pledges from secretaries to not go back to motels with their bosses, revelations of electoral fraud, declarations by men and women who had amassed fortunes pretending to be spiritualists. Irreconcilable enemies for periods of five years searched for each other in the crowd and with hugs and repentance, kissed each other. Murderers, weeping, knelt before widows whose husbands they had killed.

Many, stretched out in the form of a cross, kissed the ground in silent expiation of their sins. In front of crosses, statues of Christ, pressed against the debris, old men and women beat their breasts and whispered their sins. The sea, now an uncontrollable wild beast, continued roaring; more threatening each moment. The air and the earth trembled; it seemed like the end of the world; there was no sight of salvation.

On basketball courts and football fields, in markets, in the squares, the suburbs, barracks, schools and colleges, discotheques and restaurants, in the shoemaker shops, fathers and mothers desperately searched for their children. Screams traversed the city from one end to the other. The sea was dressed in a variety of colours and, as if a powerful magnetic force had suctioned up a part of it, its level decreased. The river became a plateau. The crowd screamed on seeing such an unusual spectacle and fled, terrified, to the hills. A voice rose from among the crowd, a voice of desperation, a convulsive wail. I ran with my parents towards the cries. There, beneath the remains of a brick wall, lay Marvin Mann's wife. A group using bars and sticks was trying to free her. Margarita was weeping beside her mother. Hurriedly, Jaime was attempting to help in the rescue. Marvin and papa went in search of a doctor, but the streets of the city had changed their positions and at first they could not find their way. Mama brought a sheet with my initials to cover her but little by little she was losing her strength. She spoke to her daughter, stuttering. Now free, she was embraced by her children and they prayed to God to save her. Ruth was pale; she had lost a lot of blood. Mama fearful that she was passing away, prayed for her: "God of mercy who, by the immensity of your compassion, erases the sins of those who repent and pardons their wrong-doings, look at your servant, Ruth Sánchez, and grant her the remission of all her sins, through our Lord, Jesus Christ. Amen."

The people, desiring to witness the stages of death, formed a circle so as to see how her life ebbed away slowly. Mrs. Mann trembled, covered with my sheet. Margarita stroked her mother's forehead while those standing around shed tears and moaned. With another quake, the group dispersed; the curious ones now ran towards the sacred image and continued confessing their sins.

Mrs. Mann did not exude her customary French fragrances as now her body emitted its posthumous vapours. I took advantage of the doctor's arrival to go in search of Ruperto. I didn't go very far as I feared another quake but I didn't see him. I went as far as the beauty parlour to find out about Manolo's condition and to check if he had seen my boyfriend. I found him crying. The showcases with the creams, facemasks, tints, nail polish and setting lotions were all broken. "You should have heard how my things sounded – chililin, chililin."

He hadn't seen Ruperto. In the early hours of the night the radio stations of other cities announced the incident. Several houses were split and roofless, others crumpled to the ground. The stands of the stadium, the Governor's office, the town hall, two schools, a wing of the hospital, fifteen light posts and the lighthouse had all been destroyed. The island facing the city was inundated; some residents drowned; the shacks disappeared. The concrete building that housed the Banco El Porvenir withstood the quakes and only suffered superficial cracks.

The body of Ruth Sánchez de Mann lay in state in the partially destroyed chapel of the Holy Trinity College. Because of the make-up that Margarita asked me to apply, she looked alive. All that was left was for her to get up and talk. She seemed to me to be taking a nap but on looking at her closely, she seemed a vain and arrogant person, one of those who believe themselves to be eternal, invulnerable to the assaults of death. The rigidity of the marble face, even when placed like this in an unpainted coffin, exuded her pride, her defiance of eternity, of the place, of the circumstances. Margarita dressed her in her bridal gown, the one she wore for her marriage to Marvin and placed in her hand a bouquet of orange blossoms.

Everybody from the district slept in the hallways. Papa took off the mattress from his bed and the three of us rested there. I kept thinking about Ruperto. For moments during my wakefulness the scene appeared when he hit me. Nevertheless I prayed to God that nothing had happened to him.

During Ruth's wake, Marvin and his children went from one side to the other accepting condolences and seating the persons who arrived, all of them still fearful of new quakes. Marvin sat opposite me and for an instance his eyes rested on my face. I felt something strange. No one had ever looked at me with an expression of such deep love. I thought that Ruth's death had provoked in him positive reactions, that he did not mourn her passing but accepted it as a normal process of life.

On the following afternoon after the religious ceremony, the coffin was transported to the cemetery on the shoulders of friends, but another tremor dispersed most of the escorts and they jumped over fissures which opened up unexpectedly.

At Margarita's wish, the casket was taken to the institutions which Ruth had headed: the Welfare Society, the Banco El Porvenir, the Pyramid Centre, the Red Cross, the Orchid Club, the Book Club, the Reporters Club, the Society of Foreign Couples.

In our house everything was in disarray. The repeated tremors had thrown to the ground the dishes, lamps, mirrors. We separated what we could use and threw out the rest in cardboard boxes. Mama went to check on her rooster; it looked at her, frightened. Very quickly I tidied the living room believing that Ruperto would come at any moment. Tired of waiting, I looked over the balcony.

Job came to my mind and I considered the passage about his resignation, one of the most beautiful in the Bible. I was dozing when I heard the voice of Luz Argentina's mother. She asked for her daughter. She had gone out to search for her at the hospital, the clinics, the Red Cross, the stadium, the park, the market but no one could give her information. I ran downstairs thinking only of Ruperto and as I thought of him my eyes filled with tears.

Stricken with anguish I reached the hotel. The staircase was destroyed, the lamps on the floor, the reception area was in shambles. They told me he paid the bill and left with his luggage and a young black girl who was wearing green lycra.

My senses became confused. The roads seemed filled with debris and darkness. I revelled in my sleepless martyrdom. I tried to rationalize the behaviour of Ruperto and Luz Argentina and I felt the roots of hate growing within me. Entangled in my own labyrinths, I sought an opening that would lighten my darkness but all my attempts were fruitless. In the depth of my thoughts I began to fashion a man, black, twenty years older than I, taller. I bestowed on him qualities of my choosing but immediately Ruperto would appear. I wanted to delve into his past, everything that he loved. I closed my eyes and in my mind I went to him with open arms; I stroked his hair; his lips pronounced pardons and excuses which hushed my complaints and helped me to forget my bitterness. Every night I created imaginary situations which now I understand were pretexts to cushion my suffering because, without such efforts, I would not have survived. Work in the bank was therapy. The bank extended more credit to assist with the reconstruction of the area affected by the earthquake. The customers, now more numerous, caused us to work extra hours. I had lunch with Margarita and her secretary in a restaurant close to the bank and she consoled me.

"Don't cry, Susana; a better young man will soon come along."

On weekends I would go to Manolo's salon so he could rejuvenate my skin which was becoming withered. He also wanted to console me. "I had a foreign boyfriend who went away to Paris. He smelled of all the fragrances. How I wept."

Early one morning, I sang to the moon until I fell asleep with my head on my *guitarra*. In my dream I saw myself talking to Nelson Mandela. He asked me if Ruperto had abandoned me because I was black or if I rejected him because he was not black. I thought that Ruperto had left me because I sang to the moon, because I would write poems and stick them unto a card with sketchings of couples who were kissing.

I spent my sleepless hours reading biographies and stories because I loved to make my imagination soar. I only knew how to prepare chocolate drink and limeade. Papa taught me to make chocolate in memory of my grandfather Mateo. I loved to dance *la Momposina, salsa, meneíto, merengue* and *cumbia*. In this way, I created bridges that linked me with other types of pleasure, other countries, other languages. I also confess that I like to whistle while I urinate, another act that makes me feel free. I confess to having had erotic dreams on nights when the moon was full and on Fridays, which for me had a flavour of Saturdays, those days when my parents stayed in bed romping, I wondered why my mother's bursts of laughter were cut short. I yearned for men – tall men, hefty men, macho men. In my imagination, I brought them to my bed so that they could make me laugh also. I confess that I never mentioned this sin of sexless love, of smiling love, wishful love. I confess my love of flowers, especially my love of trees, grass, my pleasure in bathing naked in the river and going naked on the terrace because it reminds me of my parents' peasant roots. I confess that I like freshly made cheese with roasted plantain and limeade with brown sugar.

Papa used to bring us cocoa pods. We would open them. He would place them in the sun and roast them in an earthenware pot and then peel them. Mama pounded them and after kneading, shaped them into bars. Each liquified bar made two aromatic cups, an equal number of intoxications, which led to sleep.

Papa reminisced about grandfather Mateo. He described him with his machete at his waist and straw hat to protect him from the sun. It was the era of the Great Cocoa. Each sip brought him an episode in the life of the grandparents and gave him reason to reconstruct the History that history overlooks. With the aromas more and more exquisite, papa would repeat his father's words when he spoke of the life of his employers. He was taller than she; she was fatter than he; his name was Clement Pino; hers was Ofelia Seminario; they had no children but she had two brothers. Everything smelled of cocoa: the air, new born children, nursing babies, the banks, showers of rain, women giving birth, houses, honeymoon, the stores, the animals, the sun weeping, the street, the mountains. It was a smell that in part went away on the big ships. Mateo dug holes to sow the cocoa seeds. Everything was amazing on the cocoa plantations. On doña Ofelia's fingers, diamonds sparkled; from her neck hung necklaces of gold, emeralds, diamonds and on the plantations, the labourers breastfed their babies while harvesting cocoa.

It was the era when the sweetness and aroma of Ecuadorian cocoa was disseminated throughout the world. The owners felt pains in their hands from counting money; the trucks couldn't hold the pounds sterling and the dollars; the currencies of all the countries whirled deliriously before the Great Cocoa. Doña Ofelia's brothers went to reside in France where they purchased titles of Marquis and Counts. They desperately squandered the foreign funds oblivious to the fact that the sun also sets. Doña

Ofelia bought houses throughout the country. She had two near the port and four in the city. She went to reside in Paris where her brothers lived, lost among thousands of superior faces. Each one enjoyed the gold from his plantations; each one enjoyed himself in unimaginable ways. Maybe one day they walked on the streets together without recognizing each other. There they sampled refined oriental forms of love. Perhaps when they were dancing in the salons of Europe and rubbed against the exotic breasts and felt their throbs, their thoughts momentarily would travel to their estates and they would see their cocoa trees swaying in the wind.

In Paris, they were completely transformed and little by little the Pino family forgot its three 'Early Rules': Eat Early, Sleep Early, Rise Early – the peasants' philosophy for a long life. They learned behaviour never dreamed of. They gave themselves up to the delights of Paris. Not they alone but the other cocoa plantation owners as well. The fruit gave them halos of power as if they were new gods. It gave them greatness which allowed them to hobnob with professionals, artists, beautiful women; all of who made them idolized Paris. The City of Light caressed their crotches and the bars, restaurants, theatres, dance halls, the brothels, the cabarets made them great persons. Their rise from simple mountain folk to individuals who learned the French language and European customs, who wore tailcoats and patent leather shoes and sampled cosmopolitan food caused the Great Cocoa barons to be dazzled by the fatuous fires of what was foreign, even to the point of saying that love could only be learned in Paris.

The cocoa barons spoke of their plantations across the sea, of the number of slaves, and repeated *'cacao cacao'* with a French accent. They smiled with satisfaction as they taught geography and conquered beautiful damsels. These were the days when dollar bills were used to heat tea on winter nights, tea served in gold cups by uniformed maids; the days when cocoa put the national currency on par with the dollar and became a magic wand or a new Aladdin's Lamp. The mansions of the cocoa barons were so overstocked with luxuries that they didn't see that on the plantations the anopheles mosquitoes pierced the skin of the workers and made it yellow, that their rural lips trembled from the fever. Words, truncated because of delirium, had unusual meanings and the smell of cocoa saturated the air. The day workers lived in huts without walls and with bare feet went to the mountains to sow and reap the 'gold nuggets'. They were bitten by snakes or they drowned in the fords of the rivers.

My grandparents were sowers on an estate owned by the Pino Seminario family. They cut down the forest, cleared the land with fire and dug holes in the land for the seeds. It took seven years for a tree to bear but if the land was virgin, it would produce in five. The peasants ate bananas and tropical fruits, which they planted among the cocoa trees as they needed shade. Their diet was peas, rice, corn, broad beans, fish, wild meat.

Papa went away and brought doña Ofelia Seminario. They arrived at midday. She had fixed her sparse hair in braids. She thought she would die from joy on returning to the house where she lived with her husband in the good days. So as not to look unattractive she had put on a long gown from the previous century.

"Thanks to God and to you Mateo," she said. Doña Ofelia still had some appealing characteristics. She would dress up as if she were going to a *fiesta*. She bathed every day, shined her shoes and held her cup and cutlery in an aristocratic way. She taught me to handle a knife and fork and not to put my elbows on the table. She collected empty bottles, firm in her belief that they had contained French perfumes, English lotions, bubble bath from Holland. Her arrival made it easier for me to forget Ruperto. When I didn't have classes at the university we would play cards and I remembered Grandma Matilde when I looked at doña Ofelia's wrinkles. At times, we would interrupt the card games to listen to her recollections of her brothers, of the plantations and of those golden days. During the conversations she was a dust-covered book, opened. She told the story of the first owners of the house in which we now lived.

Mr. Salaverri from Peru built it. He married Rosa Suárez and they had three children. Cesarina, the oldest, married a Paredes and he bought the house from the persons who inherited it. But Cesarina died in childbirth and Paredes married Clementina Paz. The new wife kicked out the Salaverri Suárez family. Paredes sold me this house, I remodelled it and then gave it as a gift to Mateo who was one of my good overseers, she explained.

Papa recounted the tragedy of November 15, 1922 when the police and the army killed more than two thousand persons in Guayaquil during the presidency of José Luis Tamayo, because of the oppressive poverty caused by the bankruptcy of the cocoa industry.

Doña Ofelia added that it was one José Vicente Trujillo, an emerald trader and lawyer for the Unions of the Light and Electric Company and for the Tramcar Company, and one Carlos Puig Vilazar, lawyer for the railroad workers, who incited the workers. On the 13th, the general strike began according to the regulation of the Federation of Workers of Guayas and the city was plunged into darkness. I remembered it because I almost fell on the stairs and I cursed the irresponsible workers. On the 15th of November, Trujillo spoke from the balcony of the Guayaquil Clinic so that they would set free some friends who were imprisoned. That man had a gift for convincing people. The entire group of demonstrators went towards Olmedo Avenue and the massacre started. Yes, I remember because we closed the windows and doors. I remember a black woman named Julia who protected her companions by waving the national flag and so the soldiers did not shoot. In this way she saved their lives.

On another occasion she was lucid and I was amazed at the clarity of her recollections. We stopped the game to listen: With the salary advance we would give the workers, they would buy shirts, pants, dresses imported from Europe. When I asked her why they bought European clothes, she explained that there were no national industries so all the money went abroad. Mirrors, dishes, chamber pots, spoons, powder, creams, perfumes, fabric came from abroad. And when my curiosity prompted me to find out about the chocolate bars, she replied, "They also came from Europe and the United States". Her two brothers disappeared. They never remembered her or their country. She never found out what happened to them but at times her condition worsened and she expected them to return and to contract sowers of cocoa again, forgetting that their plantations, houses, cattle were already sold. She also forgot that when the cocoa plantations were lashed by the witches' broom, the *nouveaux riches*, including herself, returned to the country. When her memory was clear she would remember the sowers and reapers, half men, half cocoa, looking more like trees than like men. The Great Cocoa planters, in their voluntary uprooting forgot the colour and warmth of their country. They forgot the fauna, the sea, the rivers, their friends. And in Paris all they remembered of the flora was their forests, full of cocoa.

When her vision cleared, her gaze would involuntarily fall on our black faces. She would avert her eyes and remain silent for hours and with an expression of shame, she would lower her voice. She would get up, dragging her feet. She would comb her thin white braids, refuse food on the pretext of having no appetite and would begin to understand the grief that accompanies catastrophes. The three of us shared her nightmare. Perhaps she said to herself, "If this family were of my own blood or my social class, the charity I receive from them now would not be so humiliating for me."

When she heard me singing a waltz she would seek my company, silent. Her consternation was so profound that tears would well up in her honey-coloured eyes and roll down her wrinkled cheeks. I would look at doña Ofelia and have the impression that she was not there, that she was only a shadow. Sometimes when she inclined her head, I would slip away, slowly, so as not to disturb her memories.

Grief did not make Marvin forget his binoculars. He delighted in gazing at Susana. It was the antidote for his sadness. He was satisfied with the way things were going. Now he slept without worry; now he was free of the apprehension of being close to Ruth with whom he feigned happiness. Now he slept without tossing in bed, trying to clutch at sleep. Nevertheless, he behaved discreetly so as not to arouse the jealousy of Margarita and Jaime. He knew very well that once they found out the truth, they would not accept another marriage for him. His daughter had imposed very rigid constraints under the pretext that he shouldn't lack anything. It was an imposition he detested but put up with for the sake of harmony. Margarita had intensified the protection of her father because now that she didn't have Ruth's alliance, her purpose was to keep the memory of Ruth intact. So that her father would continue feeling Ruth's presence, Margarita arranged for everything in the house to remain just as her mother had left it. Marvin was waiting until a year after Ruth's death to declare his love for Susana. It was difficult for him to endure it for longer, now that his wait was not as uncertain as before. Never had he felt happiness so close. His thoughts, now renewed, flowed, everything seemed easy to him. Soon, he would have a virgin that he could touch, in his bed.

He often remembered his life with his parents and his brother José and his travels through Europe. He remembered Ruth in Paris and the journey to reach the port, but his evocations were always linked to Susana. His children, now adults, wouldn't be an obstacle in his plans for a new marriage. He believed that a year was too long to wait; half a year was sufficient but afterwards he said to himself, 'one month, no longer'.

Silence surrounded Marvin, a silence full of peace that invited him to dream. His body was rejuvenated and he was now agile and performed his exercise with more gusto. He jumped out of the shower and while he was getting dressed it occurred to him that he should suggest a trip abroad to his children. It would be a period of relaxation. They had suffered so much because of Ruth's death that a change of environment was the best thing. They would visit relatives in the United States. Margarita smiled at the idea and thanked her father with a kiss on his forehead. Jaime refused to travel because he was attending university.

A month after Ruth's death, the Cathedral bells announced a mass for the repose of her soul. The religious service was attended by civil authorities, the military, clergymen and representatives of the highest level of the bank and the society. Sitting with my colleagues from the bank I noticed that Marvin, instead of concentrating on the ceremony, was looking at me intently. It was the first time in so many years of knowing him that he had looked at me in that way. He was wearing white shirt and pants. In his eyes was the splendour of the sea at five in the afternoon. His lips had a fixed smile as if he were saying, "The King is dead, long live the King!" His happiness did not go unnoticed by the rest of the guests who were aware of his personality from the time he arrived in our country. Some persons assumed that in his country sadness was not expressed, that a person brought up abroad had a different concept of death. The people who attended the mass, when they saw Mr. Mann's rejuvenation, murmured that some secret had given him back his joy because the change in his appearance was so noticeable. Some magic had changed the expression in his eyes and his face had an amazing expression of euphoria. Now he would lean forward in a youthful greeting and his cordiality to those who attended was evident. I was surprised that when he was leaving the Church he unnecessarily brought his lips close to my right cheek and thanked me for attending, leaving me with a good amount of his perfume. I pondered, what will Mr. Mann do now that he is a widower? When the mass ended, Margarita went to the airport to leave for the United States where her grandmother, Mary Mann, resided.

In the afternoon Marvin arranged for me to come to his office. Another fear danced in my mind. Could he have suspected the plan for the hold-up? In my desire to be prepared to answer his questions, I felt that time was racing along but I controlled my distress. Perhaps there was an error? I waited for a second directive, as I wanted to be sure that I was really the person who should present herself to management, or maybe he only wanted to check on some account or document. Why did his order coincide with Margarita's absence? She had been my friend since childhood. She got me the job. She was my solace.

"Would Miss Susana Garcés come to my office, please?"

"Yemayá, save me!"

I closed my cashbox and ran to the bathroom. I whistled slowly. The shock could be strong. I should prepare myself so I wouldn't wet my panties. I looked at myself in the mirror. It reflected my terror but a terror that made my face glow. If he accused me of having some part in the attempted bank hold-up, I would deny it. I haven't seen anything; I haven't heard anything. I don't know anything. If Ruperto say something that would really mess me up – but I don't think he's that stupid – I know nothing about the hold-up. I have never known anything.

When I entered, he made a gesture as if to say, "You have come at last!" In front of him, I bowed my head slightly. I noticed that he looked at me like a tiger stalking its prey. He offered me a seat and I crossed my legs, involuntarily leaving a part of my thighs exposed. He couldn't conceal the continuous struggle that he had where I was concerned. Inside me, I felt my fear crumbling. I smiled and he smiled also. What was happening to me? What was happening to us? He must have asked himself if he would have the good fortune of getting me in his bed. He wasn't to be blamed for having loved me since I was a little girl. Life was to blame for having put us on the same path.

He spied on her from the terrace, touching her uncovered breasts with his eyes. Afterwards, when she was naked he kissed her body centimetre by centimetre. She would slap her bottom lightly; sometimes she would take a eucalyptus branch to slap her back and thighs. She would lift her legs one at a time to make it easier. She would pour water from a gourd and soap her plump body. In this way, he came to know Susana's body by memory.

"Do you want to be my secretary?" he asked after a long pause. I couldn't reply to him; I felt my jaws clamp shut. Could I be dreaming? Of his own free will he would have me by his side so that I could learn the secrets of his work and the ins and outs of his business. Why me? I must have been as pale as death as he offered me a glass of water. I swallowed some. Once again, our smiles coincided and our eyes met when I told him, "Yes, that's nice, that it's a..."; the words stuck in my throat.

The next day the procedures practised by Marvin and Susana began to change. Her cashier's window was replaced by a large office and she began to get acquainted with the internal working of the bank, its gears, pulleys, its confidential accounts, the vault which housed the assets and the foreign exchange as well as international relations. She thought of Ruperto. What if he knew where I've reached?

It seemed natural to everybody in the bank that Susana, a law student, should be the manager's secretary. For him, the new office was the threshold of his plan where he felt like a teacher who was imparting all his knowledge to that student. He dictated letters to her, trying to make each task a love poem. Susana was excellent in that she allowed herself to be led and when the day ended she would sigh, half closing her eyes. Marvin noticed that he was getting closer to her, that he was making strides towards his goal, that soon they would be in tandem on the path to love.

They extended their hours of work and as his influence on her increased he healed the wounds created by Ruperto and Luz Argentina. He changed her habits one by one. Instead of a soda, Susana now had grapefruit juice; instead of pastry, she now preferred an apple. Before, he would work with the lights on, now they stayed in semi-darkness. His personality changed because of Susana's good humour and when she smiled, she was like a surprised child. But both of them knew that the walls that existed between them, high and solid walls, would require colossal strength to be demolished. Susana attended to the mail without looking at the blue of his eyes. When she didn't know the code for an account, Marvin would come close to her and when the young girl felt his breath so close to her face, she trembled.

I was in the post for only one week and was already a mad woman because only a mad woman could think about what I thought about. When I looked at myself in the mirror I came to the conclusion that Marvin and I were in the same position because it wasn't sane for him to stare at me so intently when I was writing letters. Wasn't it madness to have taken me on as his secretary without consulting his daughter Margarita, his right hand¿ Wasn't it insanity on my part to have accepted the post¿ Good Heavens! We were two lunatics who knew quite well what they were doing. He drafted business letters for me using unusual expressions. When I asked for explanations, he bent his head so close to my cheek that I felt his face almost rubbing against mine and in a persuasive voice he showed me the correct version. I ended up obeying him but he never sent those letters to anyone. He kept them at the bottom of his desk. With that deliberate way of talking, so authoritative, serious, he always sought my opinion to solve whatever he could contrive. I made comparisons with Ruperto and in every way Marvin came out superior. I was surprised. There was no teacher that with just one explanation could make the student assimilate the lesson. When I was in the classes for law, international issues or statutes, Marvin would appear in my thoughts as my teacher who understood everything. I felt my heart beat rapidly and then what I wanted was to return to the office as soon as possible.

And Marvin felt a kind of fire burning in his heart, a desire, each time more urgent to have a young virgin in his bed, at long last a virgin, a decent girl, young and beautiful. Susana, intelligent, Susana sweet and modest, Susana with her narrow waist and firm buttocks. Her parents were hardworking, religious and knew how to play chess. Susana, his sweet little rabbit. She was all the woman he knew and those he never knew; she alone, with such juicy flesh.

On Saturdays Marvin would come punctually to play chess with papa. I concluded that Ruth's death had given him a better understanding of life, a broader perspective. I wasn't aware of the moment when I made him a part of my home life, taking him out of the office. I started to speak about him to my parents and to doña Ofelia. I cleaned the terrace, the kitchen, the dining room, the balcony, whispering his name. In my mind, he would come to my bedroom and he stayed with me even in my sleep. I liked his habits, the way he spoke, his signature, the way he held his gold Parker pen, the way he wiped his sweat. He saw an opportunity for my company at snacktime and he took advantage of those breaks to exchange ideas about pending matters. He changed his white shirts for others with brighter colours. He used a more fashionable cologne and he arranged to record *salsa* and *merengue* music played by an orchestra. He told the office attendant to put flowers on my desk every day. I wondered, could it have been he who sent me flowers like those every Friday? I couldn't answer my question. He was attentive to my smallest wishes. He gave the impression of having recently discovered the desire to live. I felt as if he were absorbing me sip by sip. When the work was finished, he made me stay to listen to him reading poems. He declared that the office routine robbed him of his pleasure. On occasion, I would contradict persons whose ideas I found unacceptable because their treatment of the topic lacked depth. With flushed cheeks, he finally acknowledged that I was right. "You are intelligent", and I was riding on the train of excitement.

It was the time when the bank chose its queen. The contestants paraded in casual clothes and the event would take place on a weekend morning in the complex that the bank owned on the outskirts of the city. That Sunday wasn't just any day for Marvin. He went very early to the barber so he could get a Marlon Brando hair cut. He went to the store, Busy Corner, where they told him that clothes, especially for young people, were sold. He got a brand name sports outfit and stylish dark glasses to prevent wrinkles from the sun. Susana was surprised to see Mr. Mann in the hall of her house because just at that moment she was coming out of the bath and only a towel covered her body. He was transfixed and made an effort not to embrace her. The air was filled with a fragrance that he felt was intoxicating him. He caught a glimpse of the outline of her curves because the damp towel clung to her buttocks. They apologized to each other. He wanted to take her to the contest in his car.

Now he thought only of Susana and he had no intention of giving her up even if Margarita begged him on her knees to do so. He felt that he was too helpless to be able to give up that pleasure. Susana was a virgin and this led him to reflect deeply. He had fulfilled his obligations to his children; they didn't need him; they could live on their own. He felt he had adequate justification for his position. He closed his eyes to better capture the image he had recently seen. He caressed her mentally like a landscape or a symphony. Susana went into her bedroom to get dressed and when she appeared she had her *guitarra* under her arm.

While they were on their way to the sports complex, he

became more acutely aware of Susana's virginal aroma. It was her skin that produced that aroma. He was happy because she was smiling. Suddenly Susana became meditative. The memory of Ruperto disturbed her. It was difficult for her to put aside that memory which, evening after evening came to her like a nightmare. Marvin opened a box of chocolate-covered almonds and offered it to her. The car jerked suddenly when Marvin swerved to avoid a dog, scattering the sweets all over the rug of the car and Susana laughed, revealing her teeth.

He was startled; on seeing her laugh he pressed his legs together, remembering the solitary pleasures of adolescence. While they were driving along he asked her to sing and she sang softly:

My life is hanging by a rose because...

While he listened to her, Marvin wondered if he would be brave enough to face his children if he should marry her. It was an emotional struggle because he felt that he couldn't choose between the love of a woman who gave him strength to live and his paternal love for Margarita and Jaime. The fear that Susana would not be accepted by them paralysed him. But, how could he escape from this young girl who was driving him crazy¿ His was a love that seemed centuries old, that existed before time, before he existed and it was boundless. If Susana rejected him, he would have no reason to continue living. He stared at the road, lost in thought. He should make a decision before proposing to her. But when he thought of not seeing her anymore, if she rejected him, he sank into a depression he had never experienced before. He covered his face with his hands and the car went out of control for a moment.

"Oh, you want to kill me."

"I would never commit such a crime."

Marvin continued struggling with his doubts. His children would not accept a stepmother and worse, she was black, but at that moment he was prepared to fight to the end. He would not be afraid of his children. There was no time to waste; he was determined; he would marry Susana, if she accepted his proposal.

When they arrived the participants were waiting. Only unmarried employees could compete for the title. Susana was number five and Marvin was responsible for taking the card out of the box. He put in his hand, announced five and quickly put the card in the container. And everybody saw the boss' clever move but they applauded Miss Garcés' victory. She was excited at having won and thanked them effusively. She entertained them on the *guitarra* backed by a group of employees.

Marvin drank whisky and was moved to recite some verses of "Ode to the Horse". In fact, he would never again commit such an affront to poetry but at that moment he had to have a drink in order to be brave. Why wait¿ He saw the urgency for his marriage. He would take advantage of Margarita's absence. He needed to kiss the lips of his queen, her lips in particular. It was a sign of conquest and he wanted to have her with him forever. It was a question of honour, a challenge to his manhood and he was anxious to secure his future and his old age.

The alcohol made him brave. He stopped thinking of Margarita and went to where Susana was singing with her colleagues. He felt ageless, full of energy to start again. The liquor made all his doubts evaporate and his uncertainty about getting Susana became a thing of the past. He looked at her with the composure of a person who is certain of victory. He requested silence. He would announce that he loved Susana. But no one paid him any attention, as they were all drunk.

Three days remained for me to continue working as Marvin's secretary. I was aware that it wasn't cowardice to run from danger and before I could be sucked into the vortex I would resign from the job. He would have assured me of professional success, without doubt. Enjoying his confidence and having graduated as a lawyer, perhaps I would have worked at the same company. From Marvin, I learned the courtesies required to deal with the public. I learned how to handle matters wisely and discreetly. But I decided to leave the bank. At times when he pretended to read, I felt his eyes scrutinizing my gestures, my expressions, my way of holding a pen, of sitting and standing.

Talking to Marvin was good for me because of the security that he exuded. He continued to pull me out of the corner of hate in which I was agonizing. I was a piece of clay to which he was giving shape, the shape he desired. In this way, we were both recreated.

When there was a lot of correspondence, enquiries, interviews, telephone calls, I would run from one office to another taking appropriate responses. I collaborated in the solution of a problem and then he would congratulate me on my competence. When the tasks were completed, he praised my vitality, my youth, my attitude to life.

Two days prior to the date of Margarita's arrival, I observed that he was distressed. He was powerless to protect and defend his euphoria. He was frightened of his daughter's personality and his preoccupation was visible. On the eve of her return, he awaited the call that she would make to him informing him of her arrival. Seated at his desk, he tried to read what his mind did not understand. He continued signing documents but was unable to hide his concern. Seeing him like that, like a motionless shadow with his serenity aborted, moved me to pity. He looked like a big child who was punished and he had a guilt complex that made his throat constrict. He retired early on the pretext of a meeting. He said he would return later and stumbled as he opened the door.

When he returned he was disturbed and hardly looked at me. I realized that Marvin's weak point was Margarita but I saw her as fragile, like a vulnerable porcelain figurine. Why was he so afraid of her? There was a feeling of doom. It was difficult to work with a boss who was governed by remote control by his daughter. I recalled when papa took me to the puppet show. Hanging by their necks, the puppets responded to the manipulations of their owners. I was in time. I wouldn't work anymore as Marvin's secretary because he had to change so much. I compared him to an old house that required changes to its structure and its windows. The ceiling, walls and columns needed to be repaired. It had to be remodelled or it would collapse. He would be happy if he were free of his daughter, his confidante. He couldn't live without her help or perhaps it was the opposite, he couldn't live with it. Just thinking of Margarita's return made his voice tremulous. His hands shook, his steps were faltering, he paced back and forth in his office and he mopped his face constantly.

The telephone rang and he looked at me with dilated pupils as if he had entered a lion's den. Why was Marvin so overpowered by fear¿ Because of the shattered expression on my boss' face, the idea came to me that Margarita, in spite of her appearance, was a rare specimen, although I believed her father was exaggerating the extent. I realized that he wanted to have me at his side, to speak to someone who knew how to listen to him, a woman prepared to accept him as he was. I deduced that he had never been happy and he had a profound need to share his concern and tenderness with someone. The telephone continued ringing. It must be the call he was expecting. I answered, "One moment, please..." It's Margarita, I told him.

On the other end of the line she asked whose was the female voice. He withdrew into himself and a fit of coughing shook him. Marvin had no privacy; she would check his movements, his acts, his thoughts and she would make a mental inventory every day, even from a long distance. I saw bitterness in his eyes and his words. I saw that he wanted to quickly end the conversation. I kept quiet and decided to leave the room so that he could talk without me there but he made a sign for me to wait. Something incredible happened. His cheeks took on the look of the sea in summer and I recalled the changes in Dr. Jekyl and Mr. Hyde. I stayed there, waiting. I didn't believe it: my boss had suffered a metamorphosis. His fallen countenance was transformed into a youthful smile, with a desire to live. With his eyes sparkling, he looked handsome enough for me to fall in love with him.

"You can stay as long as you want."

He hung up the phone and to my surprise he took me by my waist and lifted me up. I couldn't react. He was a mad man passionately excited as if the door of the cage in which he was enclosed had been opened for him. I went quickly towards the park and he came after me and sat by my side. He looked into my eyes and said, "Marry me."

We both agreed to be discreet and we carried out the preparation for the wedding as if we were planning a hold-up with the utmost secrecy since neither Margarita nor Jaime would understand or accept that their father had been attracted to a black girl like me. They would not support the replacement of their mother, a white high-society lady, who gave talks in intellectual centres as well as for charity, with a poor little girl. For them, it would be impudence to carry through such a plan. Their father would have to be mad. I suggested to Marvin that he tell them the truth but he dismissed the possibility of a conversation with them. I couldn't work out what type of relationship I would have with my stepchildren. At first I believed I would be a kind of sister as Jaime and I were the same age. Then I realized that as we were of different races and different social classes, I couldn't play that part. The role of friend and confidante would suit me better. I dared to think about the matter because we grew up together in the district but each idea collapsed, as I knew full well about the pride of his children. I ended up believing that it would be better to wait for their reaction. Now Marvin watched me constantly, fearful that

I would renege on the engagement because he was so many years my senior. One morning Marvin asked me to sit in his lap and though I was reluctant, I agreed. It was like disrespecting the boss but as he would be my husband shortly, I thought he was justified. He overcame my resistance and anxiously moved his hands almost brushing my body without daring to touch me. It was like torture but fascinating, an ethereal caress that made me hallucinate in the night. As the wedding approached, to his surprise, he kept discovering my charms and when he kissed me he would surrender completely to the pleasure of the moment. I noticed that for the first time he was enjoying happiness and realized that it was a feat for him to have survived with Ruth.

His excitement put him in good humour; now he laughed at everything and he realized his good fortune in finding happiness. He felt justified to ask for a vacation. We would take a trip but to avoid comments and complications, I continued going to the bank until the eve of the wedding. I wanted to be sure that it was love that I felt for him not merely childish infatuation. He remembered me with my cloth bag in which I took my articles to school. He had seen me playing basketball with Jaime and Margarita and had instilled in them affection towards me. Then he saw me wearing my school uniform with my legs long and shapely. He confessed that he had constructed the terrace just so he could see me with his binoculars. He was the one who sent me flowers every Friday and prayed to God at nights to keep me safe for him. Now he gave thanks to the Creator for having made his dream come true. He acted correctly in his home so that I wouldn't be afraid to accept him. He was virtuous in the hope that when he was compared with others, he would triumph. When he saw me sitting in the park with Ruperto he felt humiliated before God. God had punished him. Then he begged Him with more fervour to make me his. He told me this smiling and without blushing and when he confessed it to me, his eyes gleamed. When I joined the staff at the bank, he saw me in his path and he went to church to give thanks to the Almighty.

We continued preparing for the wedding as if we were playing house. Mama began to suspect something. A miracle had occurred; I was having a good time; I cried, laughed and danced. I was happy and sad but in my sadness I showed joy. I played my *guitarra* and I danced. I smelled of pine, of freshly cut grass. I knew this smell when I was engaged to Ruperto – a fresh smell, liberating, a smell of the woods, of the sea, of a full-moon night by the river.

"Good heavens, my daughter is crazy!" mama said. She came into my bedroom unexpectedly and was amazed to see me speaking to myself. She mentioned my change to doña Ofelia. She could not understand why everything around me had a glow of love. I would be married the next day.

I went to Manolo's to get my hair done and to get a manicure and pedicure. He noticed my sparkling eyes. When I was finished I asked him to be the witness at my wedding.

"Has Ruperto come back¿"

"No, I'm getting married to Marvin Mann".

The comb fell from his hands and he urgently asked for a glass of water. I arrived at the bank with my resignation and handed it to Marvin. Then I thought it was the appropriate time to speak to him about Ruth. Thoughtful, he tried to answer my questions with an affectionate nostalgia as he recalled her invented stories. He looked around him as if he were looking for Ruth and he sighed.

"My little rabbit. I love only you." He pulled me to his chest and I saw him dry his tears.

Marvin bathed early, his thoughts only on the wedding. He looked at himself in the mirror. His gray hair was concealed with dye, his wrinkles disguised with a sunblock cream. He paced the bedroom with long strides as if to show that he was still young. He encountered Jaime in the dining room. When Jaime noticed him enveloped in a cloud of perfume and his eyes gleaming with joy he asked him smiling, with whom he had a date. Marvin hesitated a moment. He couldn't tell his son that that morning he would marry Susana Garcés. A type of fear caused him to knit his brows. The father looked keenly at his son so as to penetrate his feelings. Jaime's eyes, also blue, gave the impression of two crystal balls. His straight nose and his face were freckled and this heightened his youthful appearance. He had about ten girlfriends and changed them because of stubbornness or his desires to experience other lovers. He was born with an inclination towards those women who were skilled in love. A thought crossed Marvin's mind, perhaps an intuitive thought, which shook him.

"What's wrong, father¿"

Marvin remained pensive and silent as he felt two invisible hands squeezing his neck.

The marriage took place outside the city. Manolo, holding his assistant's hand, was dressed in white. Father Rafael Savoia, a priest from Italy and a friend of papa's, blessed us. Marvin took the chance of kissing me in public and we both laughed.

When I arrived home, dressed as a bride on Marvin's arm, my parents and doña Ofelia looked at us as if in a dream. Mama, half-happy, half-sad, half-awake, half-asleep said, "Daughter, one should always choose a partner at the level of one's nose." We kept silent. Papa filled glasses with champagne that I had kept for the occasion. Doña Ofelia, her hand trembling, raised her glass to toast our happiness. Marvin felt the sensation of victory as his dream had become a reality. Manolo and his companion looked at us astounded, trying to fathom how, why and where we had fallen in love.

I looked at Marvin. He was the old man that each girl carries inside: the grandfather or father or the uncle who protects us from the ills of the world. The old man who always brings us a gift, who staves off bad luck, who forgives us a thousand times, who always treats us with tenderness. The always amusing old man who tells anecdotes. The one who is happy with a little: he is happy with his friends, with a glass of wine and a good book; who sleeps lightly, which makes him alert while we sleep.

Marvin did everything calmly, too slowly, with too much discipline. All of that was very different for me and as I did everything quickly, everything was changing. Unconsciously he clung to order and unconsciously I clung to disorder, to breaking his rules. He spoke calmly, pronouncing his words carefully whereas I used gestures to replace words. He danced the *tango,* I *merengue.* He wanted to become a part of my world; he was aware of my youth; he didn't want anything to separate us; he wanted to prolong my joy, my freshness. He was tolerant of my pranks because he thought that losing me would be to lose himself. He gave thanks to God that his desires had been granted and on the honeymoon we went to the beach to daydream and pretended not to hear:

"Look, a black girl with a white man. What a stupid white man!"

Slowly we came to understand each other, I with my craziness, he with his good sense. Now we didn't see the barriers between one and the other; our differences were imperceptible. Deliberately we forgot Margarita and Jaime in our desire to fully enjoy our delirium. One early morning a pain in my ovaries woke me. I started to cry quietly. I urgently needed a tranquilizer or I would die that morning as the menstrual pain was intense. For the first time, I confessed to him that every month I wept when I had my period. He was very surprised and covered my tears with caresses. My cries were so loud that he thought I would die. He went to the medicine chest and dissolved all the tablets he found and without the strength to ask him what it was, I took the remedy. When I woke up after eight hours he was kissing my hands.

As the honeymoon was coming to an end, his children began to creep into our thoughts. As each day passed, we spent the night with a mutual preoccupation which we concealed. He started to look at me strangely as if trying to declare something sinister. We both experienced the same emotions about the danger of facing reality. We managed not to spoil our amorous relations but he understood that my eyes were becoming sad. I wanted to know where we were going to reside and I asked him. There was a heavy silence.

"My house is big, it has Persian carpets, oil paintings, tapestry, mirrors. We'll live there."

We were about to have a quarrel but I thought of my parents. They were so happy! Yemayá, help me. The honeymoon wasn't even finished and our problems were beginning. I made him know that I did not want to live in his house, that an apartment for the two of us would be better. Marvin laughed. He explained to me that it was absurd to leave his house which had all the facilities, absurd to enclose ourselves in four walls.

If he did not accept leaving that house, it was because he really did not love me, I thought. And this thought took root in my mind. Solitude began to take hold of me. In the sky above a light appeared that was reflected in the sea but... why begin to be ungrateful¿ Ruperto appeared in the mist; I felt his fingers caressing my back and my breasts were on fire. I remembered Luz Argentina; would she be happy with him¿ I continued conjuring up those evenings when the sun was setting and she would come to my house to tell me what took place in the boutique and we would laugh. I remembered her divorced parents. I forgave Ruperto and Luz Argentina for betraying me. I was afraid of continuing to live with Marvin, of changing my home, changing my surname, changing my way of life. I felt that I had lost everything. I went for my *guitarra*. With it I became aware of the hours which seemed to me to have gone with the wind.

"I don't want to live with your children." The husky voice of the sea reached me and a fear lodged within me. He stared at me.

I raised my face and faced his gaze. "You negroes have deep hatred. From everywhere ghosts come pursuing you, making you contemptible. You are ungrateful. Margarita took you to the bank."

He intruded into my intimate world, into what runs through my veins and genes. I would have given everything I had to retrace my steps if it were possible. I felt a desire to go away from Marvin forever when I saw my dreams destroyed.

"I forbid you to say one word which would turn me against my children." While we spoke I noticed that something was burning inside me, what was most sacred to me: my parents, my grandmother, my ancestry, my history. I began to run to conceal my weeping. The waves lashed the beach; the sea became rough and its waters turned bluish green. I looked at the glittering sky. Close by a couple with two children were bathing at the edge of the beach. I believed that Marvin was a river with calm waters, a pool where I could bathe without fear of drowning, but I was mistaken. He was a sea of conflicting currents, a body of dangerous waters. Its waves would drag me into a vortex. I still had time. I would leave his side.

Marvin walked all around, to the beach, up and down the streets, to the church, the market. He went to the bedroom. He did not find me. He looked around, his eyes straying and he reacted to all his anxieties with a movement of his head, reproaching himself for his behaviour. I felt weak when I remembered his words and I spent the rest of the afternoon absorbed in my thoughts but that same worry made me feel for the pleasure of playing the *guitarra*. The owner of the bar, on recognizing me as the wife of the 'gringo', allowed a black girl to take the stage. My voice led him to the dance hall. He was distressed, with his hair dishevelled, and exhausted. He sat in front of me as I sang "La Momposina". My expression oscillated between the joy of remembering and the clouds of the moment. My voice expressed triumph but with a touch of failure. Now my skin, showing the effects of the sun, gleamed all over. He looked at the audience which was focussing on my lips. They served him a bottle of whisky. He was right to drink. He should begin to learn how to love. Perhaps he thought that I was still bound to Ruperto. I realized it that night and had to free myself. His eyes were clouded with grief. He imagined that sooner or later he would have a rival and he began to feel the discouragement that old age brings.

I pretended to sleep. He did not turn on the light so as not to awaken me. He lit two candles which were on the chest of drawers, went to the bathroom and put on his pyjamas. He rubbed cream and cologne on his cheeks and after turning around slowly several times, he got into bed.

"Little Bunny," he whispered.

"Why did you put on your pyjamas¿"

Love was spread everywhere. We had never said such things to each other. In his eyes were traces of sadness and pleading. He added that I was his happiness, his reason for living, the tenderness he had never had. He asked me to close my eyes and then I felt him place something on my navel. When I opened them, a diamond sparkled in the light of the candles. We laughed. Now there was no place in our minds for quarrels. He wanted to live in his mansion, there we would make our home, so it would be.

We started our return journey. For me it was difficult to live in the house of the deceased, in the kingdom of Margarita and Jaime, who would take up arms against the person they considered an intruder. However, I gathered my strength to smile; I presented a happy appearance so that he wouldn't be aware of my concern. Marvin was deceiving himself and tried to deceive me. He knew very well that on arriving at his house we would be confronted with the anger of his children. Margarita would be already waiting for us.

As we approached the city he started to get quiet. I felt his fear flow into me like something already familiar. Terror seized him as he thought of Margarita. At times he was like an ostrich with its head buried in the sand. Probably at that moment he was praying to God that I would never abandon him. He was frowning. I noticed his pressing desire for meditation, as if an energy more powerful than his strength imposed on him silence and concentration.

On opening the door to his home, Jaime's face emerged from the depths of the living room as I stared at his blue eyes. I accepted his courtesy receiving us with a bunch of red roses. I accepted the gift politely as father and son embraced and we shook hands. I scrutinized the dining room presuming that Margarita would be at the other end. Jaime lit the lamp that was hanging from the ceiling. The light that suddenly illuminated the book his sister had in her hands, left part of her face in the shadows. I saw her profile: she was reading; her nose straight, her blonde hair on either side of her face. I looked at her face, so familiar. She was my friend with whom I had played since I was a child, who comforted me when Ruperto fled with Luz Argentina, but now I was her stepmother.

"Come, Margarita," Marvin said. They embraced.

Suddenly I felt my cheeks burning. Courage! I mustn't become scared. She approached laughing, bedecked with jewellery. I didn't know if she was laughing at me or at her father. We shook hands and she continued laughing. Her laughter felt like a dart. Marvin put the flowers in a vase and the water fell on the carpet. Jaime dragged the suitcases to the bedroom and Margarita returned to her mother's rocking chair. I saw her bite her lips. She wants me to go, I said to myself, to leave her father, to forget him.

I tried to pretend. She looked up at the lamp where the lights were hung. Enough, I said to myself. Margarita, stop laughing. If you only knew how I longed to marry your father since I was a child and he gave us caresses and nougats. He would stop reading and bend his head forward to see me clearly. Marvin spent a good part of his life praying to God and to the Virgin for me to marry him. Leave him with me. I will care for him in his old age. I am young and could go away but I promised him to remain at his side forever.

Margarita spoke of her mother, of her importance in the society, of her discourses on Columbus Day, of the applause she received for her oratorical performances, of her white skin, of her straight blonde hair, of the set of crockery with gold at the edge which cost her so much money, of the cream she prepared from carrots. I had never felt so many daggers in a voice.

"Will your mother continue to wash our clothes¿"

I didn't answer her. I felt in that house an energy which expressed the presence of someone, not exactly a person, because it was like a slight creaking or a scratching on the walls. A noise began to move in my ears. At times I felt it as a spiral of echoes, constant, extended, similar to the nibbling of a rat. I saw the oil painting which hung above the marble table and recognized Ruth's image with her blue velvet dress, wearing a heavy necklace of emeralds and diamonds. I looked at Margarita's neck and was so surprised that she had dressed herself just like the deceased. She spoke now of Ruth's death then jumped from one topic to another with the subtle characteristics of that woman whom I was replacing. She forced me to think about her. Now I could see and feel Margarita's style. She had the same characteristics of the deceased; they flapped their words before others like flags of superiority. She was a dead woman who wasn't buried. I understood that there were dead who gave orders, dead who never die, dead who mutter their Decalogues. They seem to go away but they do not. They reappear with greater orders. I began to alienate that dead woman and, may God forgive me, I learned to hate her. It was not my intention to create discord with the deceased although at night she frightened me during my sleep, during my lovemaking, and I felt her coming to reclaim her position.

In the darkness I saw her silhouette. I heard her walking from here to there, from one place to another. In the thickness of the night, her eyes shone like fireflies. Could I adjust my life to that mansion which I felt had no air, no window, where everything was arranged according to the strictest order and with fine taste? Here a console table with a French mirror, nearby a pedestal with flowers, over there oil paintings with golden leaves. In the corners, display cabinets with porcelain figurines, everything in its place. To move even one thing would disrupt the harmonious balance of the living room. Would that ever be my living room, my dining room, my kitchen? No. First it would have to be over the dead body of my stepdaughter. That was not the love nest of which I had dreamt.

Jaime, when the day's tasks were completed, would sometimes come to say his childish goodnights and would bring nougats and a rose. I thanked him with a kiss on his forehead. I was getting accustomed to Marvin's tender love, with a sometimes melancholy sensitivity.

One night I cried out hearing the scurrying of a rat. In my wakefulness I tried to decipher the meaning. Could it be a secret longing to go away from that house? I became aware of the feeling of being watched by two bright eyes. I heard the scratching sounds on the floor, in the drawers, the corners, on the bedside tables, in the chest of drawers. Marvin went several times to search for it in the wardrobe, among the coats, hats, shoes, in vain. But I heard it moving its tail and running from one place to the other. I heard it stop to scratch its ears. I believe I saw it showing me its teeth as if it were laughing. At other times it seemed to me that I saw it scrutinizing the corners, and it stopped and turned over. One early morning I saw it open a hole in the wall and with its bright eyes it threw sharp and questioning looks at me, it would hide and then push out its head and mockingly raise a foot to lick it, performing little tricks.

It would go away and return, obviously believing that it was playing with me. I saw its shine teeth and admired their whiteness, agility, perfection. I shivered, sweated and Marvin searched for the rodent everywhere in the bedroom, concluding that the rat came from the gully where there was garbage.

As the days progressed, hope was reborn in me. I should not torment myself because of a rat. I would go close to it, caress its white velvety fur. I decided to give it a name. For a week, I considered some possibilities and made a list. I needed to choose one that harmonized with its beauty, that matched its qualities, was short and melodious. I decided to name it Toqui.

Before going to bed I called Toqui and said goodnight to her. I left the door open for her so that she could enter without making noise. When I made love with Marvin, from the doorway she raised her head to look at us. I ended up growing fond of her because Toqui made my imagination soar. She transported me to regions never before suspected. At times her gaze was empty, expressionless. At other times it was confidential and at the same time terrifying. One night Toqui moved close to the door and kept her eyes glued to my face. Her hate was eloquent. She moved her body skilfully and scratched the floor with her claws. I smiled at her, unable to calm her.

"Toqui, Toquicita," I said sweetly. She continued with her piercing looks, with her haughty pompous eyes, with her fur on edge, angrily hitting the door with her tail.

I remained seated in silence then I walked barefooted to the window. The moon was shining and the sky looked like a nearby piece of the sea. Marvin was out of the city attending the inauguration of a branch of the bank and I was surrounded by solitude. Why was I wasting my time in that house? What was my future with that rat? I decided to return to the university to continue my studies.

The lights from the light posts here and there, at that hour of the night, flickered as if they were about to go out. Business places had closed their doors and people entertained themselves watching television in a lounge where liquor was sold. That night they were broadcasting a football game between Barcelona and Emelec and the shouting could be heard two blocks away. At that hour the street was like a sad, abandoned woman but I liked it like that because it emanated an aroma of acacias. I saw Marvin at the window. Now he would read while he waited for me and after kissing me, we would go to the dining room where he had dinner ready. While we ate, he mentioned his problems at the bank with such emotion that his happiness was obvious. I told him what I learned, I told him of the next strike which they were planning, about Cleofé Quiñónez and Carlos Zambrano, my colleagues with whom I studied and prepared assignments. We discussed the invitation we received where I would play the *guitarra*. My confidences interested him because when I mentioned them to him, his eyes gleamed. At times I would go to the bank and would revise my assignments there. Afterwards we would go to the Port to dine. He had the ability to interpret the law and when he saw me studying until dawn he would bring me a cup of milk and toast. Every weekend we went to the Centro Pirámide of which he was a member and to which he had gone with Ruth. We exercised and jogged around the garden. In this way, he didn't lose hope of maintaining his virility. Twice per week we 'stoked the fire', having left behind the little joke of the honeymoon for fear that I would get fed up. I updated my wardrobe and now I wore skirts below my knees, blouses with collars and my perfume was mild. When I left for the university he would kiss me goodbye, both of us blushing with emotion. Margarita would come in the night, in this way dispelling her bitterness. Sometimes Jaime didn't sleep at home, spending the night with one of his girlfriends. Marvin nurtured the hope that with time vengeance would be forgotten.

Although we had been married for two years, Margarita still had not accepted her father's decision to get married. This consumed her and it seemed that in her life there was space for nothing but hate. She had spent all this time soaking her existence in loathing, as if this were her goal. At times Marvin would come to the university and from there we would go to a discotheque to dance. On moonlight nights I played the *guitarra* for him on the verandah while, in a voice cracked with joy, he showered me with kisses. Any tone I used would increase his happiness and so he would come close to bite my lips. Margarita, hidden behind the orchids, watched not knowing how to interrupt our extended honeymoon. That was suffocating her. She would stay in Ruth's rocking chair with a smile of reproof, repeating how ridiculous it was that her father married a black girl, that he wasn't even capable of replacing Ruth with someone similar to her. She was of the opinion that he was moving too quickly with me and that it was necessary to act as quickly as possible. Suddenly she felt a sensation of triumphant joy. She continued listening to my song until she completed her plan to eliminate the newcomer forever. She had lost so much time. It wasn't madness, she would restore the family home.

One Friday I went to the bank to see Marvin but encountered Margarita who laughed loudly on seeing me and looked at me from head to toe and I thought the scene was my imagination or a hallucination. But I laughed also and when I finished my stepdaughter had gone.

One afternoon my throat felt dry and I believed it was the start of the flu. Depressed, I stopped what I was doing, saw the gleam in Margarita's eyes and left the house for the university. I had taken some notes in my notebook. I looked at the professor, pleading. I wanted to bite my tongue, the sensation of asphyxia was choking me. My throat felt like a burning sore, the images were trembling. Cleofé became alarmed on seeing my face. I fell.

In the morning, surprised, I heard Marvin's voice in the clinic. My throat and stomach were hurting me. "My darling."

The thought that someone tried to poison me prevented him

from speaking any more. He was deeply perturbed and haggard. Afterwards he became calm. It was impossible for him to involve his children. He hung his head as if requesting clemency. I remained silent. He thought deeply and realized what I meant in his life, but who would want me dead? I was about to tell him that as long as we loved each other, I would be in danger. Mama, doña Ofelia and papa took advantage of the silence to pray before an image of Christ hanging on the wall.

During my convalescence I was cared for at my parents home. Marvin stayed with us to give me the early morning medication but the pain in my throat was sharp. Some nights doña Ofelia chatted with Marvin about Paris and the time of the cocoa barons while my parents prepared steaming cups of chocolate, cheese and roasted plantain, to serve them. After a fortnight, Grandma Matilde returned to cure the sores in my throat and stomach caused by the poison.

She told Susana that a year before she had had an accident but suddenly became silent. The granddaughter begged her to continue but her expression suggested that something mysterious had happened to her and precisely for this reason she did not want to say it to her. Faced with this resistance but making her swear not to mention it to anyone, she continued. "That morning I was riding a horse that bolted because the reins broke. It was like a dream. I was on the sand when a man spoke to me. 'Be calm, be calm, Matilde.' I wondered how he knew my name."

"Remember everything that I am going to instruct you to do."

I felt as if a thick paste glued me to the sand but I felt no pain. That man had all the races in his face: he was white, black, yellow. He said that from that moment, I had been given the miraculous gift to heal the sick of any sickness by passing my hand above them from their head to their feet, without touching them and giving them a half glass of water that I would bless. I was to use a coffee-coloured stone in the shape of a heart, with white stripes, and rub it on the part of the body where they felt pain. He said that I would find the stone on the bank opposite my house and that I should not collect any money from any sick person.

I told him that it would be better to give those powers to someone else because people would take me for a madwoman or a liar, but he ordered me to obey. He seemed even more handsome. I got up feeling no pain. He went away and I got my horse, which was waiting for me where he had thrown me and I returned home. I went to bathe and there on the bank I found the heart-shaped stone. I doubted what that man had told me, whether it was true or false, but I began to cure people and I did heal them.

Susana got up; her grandmother looked up to the sky, opened her arms and passed her hands above her granddaughter's head. She passed the stone over her throat and down to her stomach. She went for half a glass of water which she blessed and offered to Susana. Immediately, the granddaughter felt relief. Then, she went in search of her daughter to apply medicine to her hands and knees. Carlota opened her eyes like an owl when she saw that her fingers were becoming nimble. The three women free from pain or injury, hugged each other.

They repeated the syllable om, om, om, om, for twenty minutes from five o'clock each morning and placed Susana's body on the chest of drawers to correct its defects. After three days, the grandmother returned to Plenilunio as she had to help one of her pigs which would give birth at full moon.

The person responsible for the attempted poisoning was never discovered. Marvin paid the police to close the case. The *guitarra* calmed Susana's resentment until she forgot the reason for her hatred.

But Margarita would carry her vengeance with her for her entire life. It blossomed again in her undiminished zeal to take Marvin from the world in which he lived, that world created by

Susana whose perfume did not allow her to sleep. She lifted her arms to God in gratitude for having given her a miracle. She already had another plan worked out so her father would abandon Susana forever. Seated in the rocking chair, she shook her head to keep awake and said to herself. Yes, now you will go away forever.

She forced a smile when she heard her father ask his wife to tell him one of the many stories that Grandma Matilde had taught her. The wind carried the words to her, while the two of them exchanged caresses on the terrace.

> Mr. and Mrs. Rabbit lived on the mountain in a little house of straw and branches. Tiger lived on the same mountain, a little further away. Every day Mr. Rabbit went to collect seeds from the trees for the meal. One day when Mrs. Rabbit was waiting for her husband, Tiger ate him up. Mrs. Rabbit was waiting for her husband and when he did not return fright caused her to give birth to a baby rabbit. Mrs. Rabbit left him locked up and she went for the seeds but when Baby Rabbit was big, it was he who collected the seeds and left his mother locked up so that Tiger would not eat her up. When he came home he would sing:
>
> *Climbing up my hill*
> *With my stomach full*
> *Mummy, open the door for me*
> *It is I, Tinto Rabbit.*
>
> He would knock three times, bam, bam, bam, and Mrs. Rabbit would open the door for him. But one day Tiger said, "How can I eat Mrs. Rabbit¿" He waited until Tinto Rabbit left and sang the same song to her.
>
> "Aha!" said Mrs. Rabbit, "that is not my son's voice," because she recognized the coarse voice of Tiger. "You have come to eat me".

Marvin's eyes were gleaming, anxious to find out the conclusion. I saw him like a child, attentive to my words. "Go on, go on, don't stop." I continued…

> Tiger convinced the agouti to sing the verse to Mrs. Rabbit but she

realized that it was not her son's voice and did not open the door.

Then he brought his niece, Wild Turkey, and made her hide until Tinto Rabbit came in order to learn the verse and the tone of voice. He told her that he would reward her with a piece of Mrs. Rabbit. So one evening Wild Turkey sang Tinto Rabbit's song and knocked three times on the door and Tiger ate Mrs. Rabbit without giving Wild Turkey her piece and even tried to eat her too but she flew away. When Tinto Rabbit arrived he realized that Tiger had eaten up his mother. Immediately he bought a pair of earrings, high heeled shoes, a dress, a bracelet, a ring and nail polish to cover his nails. He put on make-up and dressed like a lady. He went and walked in front of Tiger's house and since he was such a 'Don Juan'...

"And what is a Don Juan¿" asked Marvin.
"A lover boy like you."
He laughed and I continued...

"Miss, come here."

She replied, "No, you want to eat me up."

Tiger replied, "Miss, I want to marry you because I am in love with you."

"I will marry you if you agree to cut off one arm"

He accepted: cut, cut, cut.

Tinto Rabbit cut off Tiger's arm and then a leg and then took off the dress.

"Uncle Tiger, recognize me. I am Baby Rabbit. You ate my father and my mother."

Uncle Tiger said, "Nephew, forgive me, forgive me."

Tinto Rabbit refused. He killed him, skinned him and smoked the meat and took it to Aunty Tiger telling her that Uncle Tiger sent it to her and that it was a smoked wild hog. Aunty Tiger ate it up.

Margarita remained seated in her mother's favourite spot and had stopped rocking so as to listen to the story. Marvin clapped and rewarded Susana with kisses. But then something unexpected happened. He looked closely at me and then said calmly that he was grateful to Luz Argentina for having gone off with Ruperto. Susana embraced him.

Jaime came home from the street and went to greet the couple. Then Marvin asked his son to sing while Susana played the *guitarra*. They performed a duet and they drank and sang ballads and songs until Carlota's rooster announced the dawn.

Susana wore blue jeans and a little perfume and was responsible for bringing the *guitarra* and some fun to get-togethers. Sometimes Marvin accompanied her and at other times she would go with Cleofé and Carlos Zambrano. During exam time she did not accept engagements so Marvin would send a note explaining the reason for her absence.

Margarita, who was arriving home earlier now, brought them aromatic water with sweet biscuits. She was getting friendly with her stepmother; she gave her perfumes saying that it was necessary to change her personal odour. Before going to bed she would say the Lord's Prayer. She withdrew from the world to devote herself to her project. She just waited on an opportunity to carry it out. Now she had obtained Carlos Zambrano's home address. Her heartbeats grew stronger as she felt free of her enemy.

When classes resumed at the university, Margarita went to the club with Carlos Zambrano. She spoke to him about business and the possibility of a job in the Banco El Porvenir. She regaled him with presents and took him to her father's home so that they could all dine together, including Susana.

The following day when Marvin put on his pyjamas, Susana thought that a life without sex made no sense. Now her husband no longer had the passionate love of those first years but believed that to sleep with legs entwined was wonderful. A telephone call took her from her meditation.

"Susana, telephone. It's Carlos Zambrano," Margarita announced. From then Carlos used that medium to make different enquires which kept her on the phone for a long time. One night, when she arrived from classes, she found Margarita with her arms around her father's neck and the stench of a rat permeated the air. Toqui had returned and was moving her paws threateningly.

I greeted them and opened the window, which was useless as the foul smell continued. I saw the affectionate embrace again and was concerned. Now Marvin lived between two loves. His love for her and his love for me and he seemed happy. Cleofé and Carlos came to the house. The parties at the university were starting up. Now Marvin was accustomed to their presence and even allowed himself to make jokes with them. On that occasion he told them a popular joke.

A sparrow hawk with a hundred quills
cannot maintain himself
but a lawyer with one quill
maintains a mistress and a wife.

All of us laughed and applauded him. Marvin drove us to the venue of the party and stayed to enjoy the programme. He was the most enthusiastic person when I played my *guitarra* and sang. On other occasions he excused himself with niceties, wished me success in my performance and left, always concerned about maintaining our good relationship. Because of this, no one suspected that my marriage would last only a few more months and that Marvin's unexpected decision would become a scandal. While I sang successfully, Margarita was triumphantly proceeding with her plan. She became more intimate with her father; she adjusted his shirt collar; she took him his slippers; she gave him juices and pastries prepared specially by her; she showered him with caresses and cleaned blotches of cream from his face. She was determined to win back her father's confidence.

Marvin began to come home late. Now he spent his free hours at his office or at the club with his friends. He arrived with his eyes red from the effects of the whisky. On weekends he left the city on some pretext or other. His silences with me were undecipherable. When I got up, he had already left without having breakfast. One night he came in with his shirt stained with lipstick. But behind those adventures he seemed to be hiding a torment which was destroying him. He shouted for the slightest reason. One morning as he was getting dressed the lotion spilled and I heard him say,

"Damn it!"

Nevertheless, I didn't dare ask him the reason for his strange behaviour. I was afraid because his anger boiled for the simplest reasons.

Margarita and Jaime gave signals that my presence in their house was unwanted. The feeling of emptiness never left me. I forgot my *guitarra*. In the house, a great silence reigned. No one replied to my greeting. When I entered the living room my stepchildren left immediately. That solitude was only interrupted by the rat. Then my fear turned to hate for those white people who insulted me without words.

I was tense and this created a feeling of anguish in me. A terror, something inexplicable, confused me and I dealt with my premonitions silently. When he was going to sleep he wrapped himself up in the sheet and turned his back to me. At dawn, I heard him breathing deeply in his sleeplessness. I clung to his love.

He was still my idol, my man. I could not resign myself to losing him. Old complexes kept surfacing and became magnified. Because of the close relationship that Marvin had with his children, I again considered myself an interloper, an obstacle in that home. Margarita and Jaime definitely cut off their affection toward me and I began to feel at the brink of abandonment. What would I do without Marvin? Who could the other woman be¿ Was she white¿ I could not continue in this isolation. I spent sleepless nights. I cried, locked in the bathroom. I made sure they did not see my tears so as to give them the pleasure of assessing my suffering. I tried to control my weeping but the sobbing continued unabated. It was my heart that was crying. In bed, I turned over and tried to shift Marvin's position to place my legs over his. He did not respond to my affection. Over several days I had been coming to the realization that Marvin's anger was serious. But how could I attempt reconciliation without humiliating myself¿ I felt embarrassed now to tell him that I had an engagement and that I was going to sing at a *fiesta* for some ship owners. I began to drink wine to calm my nerves but he was unperturbed by this and other absences. I felt my yearnings stir and rise up from within me. I missed his warmth, his arms and I was surprised at how sex had become a part of my life. In bed, I heard the noise of the rat increasingly more resounding each time. She sharpened her teeth on the wall. From the door, she spied on the bedroom. Once again, she blinked her clear eyes in the darkness like two piercing stars.

"Damn rat!"

Marvin turned on the light. I saw his scorn clearly.

"What are you waiting on to get out of my house¿ I stopped loving you because you are unfaithful."

He threw a piece of paper in my face. Trembling, I read it. 'Carlos Zambrano is Susana's lover.' I saw my dream destroyed. Everything reeked of the rat, the air, the bedroom, the living room, and Marvin also exuded Toqui's foul smell. I recognized it was the Mann family that stank.

"Get out."

In the silence I put on blue jeans and a blouse. I took the wall poster and hugged my *guitarra*. Margarita already had the hallway door open.

Susana wondered if everything that had occurred was just a nightmare, if the anonymous person was just a hallucination.

Disbelief engulfed her and she racked her brain wondering why Marvin had thrown her out of his house. She pretended to follow the bible passage that her mother read loudly. She went around the house unable to find explanations for her misfortune. Matilde came as soon as she heard the news. She would dedicate her time to that flower which lost its petals so soon. Locked in the bedroom, with their legs crossed, they began to repeat the om om om which got louder as it reverberated against the walls. Then she took her to the mirror on the chest of drawers and forced her to look at herself for a long while. That reflection would comfort her spirit, it would not discriminate against her; it would free her from prejudice and pride. By looking at herself in the mirror she would realize that she had the necessary energy to continue on alone in life and triumph. From that impartial and honest space, Susana would draw strength to struggle courageously and wisely. When her granddaughter was sure of herself, she hugged her, looked up at the sky and burst into tears. A sadness which she could not explain seized the grandmother. She cried as if she had lost her granddaughter forever or had a premonition of her death.

Marvin, depressed, returned to his house taking with him the emptiness that his children could not fill. Kneeling before the Virgin, he asked for the strength to be able to survive without Susana. At nights he thought he would go mad: the hours were unending and the weight of his years exhausted him suddenly. He began to urinate at every moment, to breathe agitatedly and his knees began to hurt him. It was as if old age had been lying in wait for him so as to declare an all-out war. He never imagined that he loved this black girl so much. The reality was that he needed something to be able to survive: she was his tonic, his rest, his motivation, his guide, his health, his complement. He thought that all his ailments would be cured if Susana returned. He felt that his spine was broken; he almost could not straighten himself.

Cleofé went to visit his friend one afternoon and to find out the reason for her absence from class. He took the decision to investigate the matter anonymously. He concluded that there must be someone interested in separating Susana from Marvin. That night Susana changed her attitude. She went to the university and prepared to begin her vindication. In her bedroom, hugging her *guitarra,* she wept because of her humiliation caused by Marvin; she wept because she couldn't live without him; she wept because her heart felt incomplete because he had conditioned her to suit him, to his level, to his tastes and his touch, but she was sure that he would come to ask her forgiveness.

Margarita opened all the windows so that the black smell would come out; she sprinkled the house with Kreso, holy water, floral scents; and as if that was not enough, she sweetened water so that the bad luck would definitely leave the house. She arranged her father's things in a different way, packed her stepmother's things and sent them to her with the concierge from the bank; but as soon as Susana received them she promised herself to regain Marvin's love.

She attended university, certain that he would come for her. She laughed again, eventually started to have drinks again so as to relieve her sadness and began to have a closer friendship with Manolo, who lost count of the times he straightened her hair, gave her manicures and pedicures and put on make-up. One day she took his advice and tattooed her eyebrows, eyes and lips and went again to the mirror to contemplate her reflection. A dazzling brilliance was the result. She forgot how she had been before and now said 'om' in the tone of 'do' and slowly went up the scale. She straightened her spine, felt new energy and swayed her body. Her heart beat faster and once again her feet moved to the rhythm of 'om'.

She went with her *guitarra* to wherever they invited her and showed off with delight her voice and her shapely legs. She knew that in reality she wasn't singing of love but of her nostalgia, of the pain of loving. Those who heard her knew that her inspiration came from the secret everyone shared: her separation from Marvin. One night she went to celebrate Cleofé's birthday with her university friends. All of them were in the same age group, which was obvious from their way of dressing, dancing, drinking. While they drank, she realized that she had assumed an age that was not hers, but Marvin's, and for the first time she became conscious of it. She went to the bathroom and when she looked in the mirror as her grandmother had shown her, she was able to appreciate her smooth skin, her brilliant eyes, her exuberance. She could appreciate that her neck was long and free from wrinkles, that her lips were sensual and she looked at herself as she had never done before. Then she muttered the words: Happiness is living the age that one is.

When she came out, all eyes focussed on her. When she danced her body patterned the movement of a snake, going from being almost on her knees, raising herself to the beat of music. Her navel moved in circles and her friends surrounded her. As the students drank, the fun increased and they mocked the Vice Chancellor, the secretary, the professors, the President of the Republic and his Ministers. Susana forgot Marvin. Afterwards the animation became general and they spoke about Tarzan's mother, and the monkey, Chita. Between the laughter and the anecdotes they named her Silver Belly. Cleofé suggested that to liven up the party each person should tell a funny joke, a motion that was unanimously approved. Susana raised her voice and said,

"Pepito asked his teacher, 'Is it true Miss, that the heart has legs¿...'"

When she finished, laughter filled the room.

Carlota waited up for her and when she saw her daughter staggering, she said,

"I told you, one should marry a man who is at the level of one's nose."

"Don't worry, Mother, don't worry, he will come to ask for forgiveness. You'll see."

Three months later, when Susana was getting the initial flirtatious remarks from a medical student with whom she had fun in the discotheque and went to the movies, Marvin was hiding behind some pine trees at the university to see her come out. One night he rubbed himself with the most exquisite lotion that he found in a store and decided to go in search of his wife.

"I will go for my Little Rabbit before the tiger eats her up," he said to himself.

The rain served as a pretext. Although the encounter was not expected, when they saw each other face to face, they mentally recalled their happy days together. Marvin hastened to say, "The rain will give you a cold."

She preferred to walk slowly and not get into the car. A month after the first encounter, Carlota said to her daughter, "I don't have space to put the flowers that Marvin is sending to you again."

Cleofé designed a plan to investigate and discover the author or authors of the anonymous note. He went to the Banco El Porvenir for a loan and asked the secretary for a list of the requirements that were necessary so that they could be attached to the loan application. She complied with the request and, with her ballpoint pen, wrote the data. Cleofé left. He confirmed the features, the letters and the colour of the ink. There was no doubt the secretary was the actual perpetrator of the act and Margarita was the intellectual author of the plot.

When Susana left the university she went with her admirer to the port, where she sang on Friday nights to audienceswhich packed the nightclub to listen to that black voice bringing the *boleros* to life. When she got home she found her husband talking with doña Ofelia, who slept in the day so as to be able to keep Mr. Mann's company. Susana went in silence to her bedroom.

But one night Marvin waited for Susana on the porch. He stretched out his arms to her and she responded.

On that occasion I arrived at the Mann's residence on Marvin's arm, with a triumphant expression, not forgetting that the bond of our love was evident. From the entrance I smelled the stink odour of the rat. Margarita accepted the challenge, confined herself in silence and Jaime in indifference. I understood that now my husband was confronting two sources of hate. Margarita sharpened her intelligence. She looked at me with arrogance and I did likewise.

In that ostensible peace, the cards were laid on the table. We would see who played better but I did not know that she had a hidden card up her sleeve.

Marvin was anxious to begin to have pleasure with me again and was fed up with the family problems. In his eyes, I read his desire to put an end to the arguments. We waited for vacation and then we left on a trip.

A shower of fireworks, flights of doves and band music from the town welcomed the tourists to the city of Latacunga. We joined the procession, joined in the celebration of the Black Mama, an evocation of the person who was the cook for the Virgin of Mercedes and helped with the liberation of the slaves. We followed the procession amidst applause and drinks of orange juice boiled with liquor which the residents of Latacunga offered to those who were present. A person speaking in a loud voice explained that the importance of the Black Mama came about because in the time of General Urbina the freedom of the slaves was promulgated and it was the Virgin who inspired the President to issue the decree on the 25th of July 1851.

A man on horseback, dressed in striking colours and wearing a mask, with large hoops in his ears and big necklaces of glass beads led the procession. In his hands he had a black doll which he moved to the rhythm of the music. The procession sang songs of praise and popular folk songs which caused loud laughter.

Behind him came the Angel of the stars, Ashanga, the Hucos, Yambada and Camisola who, with her whip, made a passage through the revellers. Marvin embraced me and we continued like this to the church, where a lady provided the information that the celebration dated back to Spain and that the Black Mama was Queen Aixa.

It was a long time since I had felt Marvin's body so close. I looked at him time and time again and was aware of my desire to laugh at Margarita and Jaime. Now I had their father attending a celebration with me. He touched my face with the caress that I was accustomed to and that I needed so much.

Nine months later, Susana gave birth to a girl who was baptised with the name Isis. They took her out for drives in the car. Marvin and Susana preferred to have her brought up under Carlota's influence and she was very tender with her.

Moconga, the daughter of Miguel Aguas and Irene Campás, accepted the invitation of the Japanese gentleman to go to the USA to study. She arrived at the residence of Kimoto and Okio. In the beginning her concepts were confused because she mixed the speech of her friends and the traditional folk food and clothing with the colouring of the furniture. The lamps and the walls intrigued her and she found the faces of the owners of the house strange. Kimoto looked at her with sympathy and with special satisfaction and his gratitude increased because it was Moconga's father who saved him from drowning in that huge river. But she was trying to live in two different worlds at the same time and did not wish to give up either of them. At the end of the month, she was filling herself up with silence. She was like a balloon that goes up and down and when inflated it goes wandering without direction, not knowing where to land. Kimoto guessed that the tension his guest experienced was normal, memories assaulted her mind; her parents' advice, the words of her friends, scenes from her country, all resounded silently inside her.

The family, who understood the difficulty of adapting, respected her nostalgia. Moconga spent hours writing letters to her friends but little by little she came back to reality and what at the beginning seemed to her to be of no interest and out of place became the custom. Now she would question Kimo, the son of the owners of the house, and she studied English 10 hours a day. The wide nostrils of the girl dilated when she revised the conjugation of the verbs. After one term the images of Moconga's friends flowered, but they were fragmented and the thoughts she previously had about studying the language were different. She was aware that she should work and enter university. It wasn't easy for her to get a job. When they saw her they wouldn't give her the position. It was Kimoto who took her to a friend's bakery. Her job was to place the bread in plastic bags, close them quickly and then put them in a box. If there was any delay or distraction the loaves of bread would pile up and fall to the floor and this would be reason for a reduction in salary. Her experience as an athlete made her limbs agile, as in her country she had practised athletics for many years and had won medals.

When she earned a fixed salary, she thanked Okio and Kimoto and left their home, deaf to their pleas that she should continue to spend nights at their residence. Now she no longer lived surrounded by magnolias and azaleas. She looked for a tiny apartment in the black district and was lucky as the sun entered through the kitchen and the play of light made the place look larger. The rays of light entered like beams and dispersed the shadows. Moconga placed a round table and two chairs in a corner of the room and after eating they served as a study. She acquired second-hand things in different places, sanded them down and applied a coat of varnish to them. She desired intensely to learn. Something flowed inside her like a current that ran below the river surface.

Moconga took lunch to work – an apple and a sandwich. The

sandwich was mostly of lettuce, considering the transparent slice of cheese that it had. At ten in the night she would arrive home, prepare hot soup, called 'Old Women's Water' in her country, which was an infusion of aromatic herbs, and sit and study until 1:00 a.m. When she passed the third year in the Faculty of Anthropology, she started to sing when she got up; she sang a song about a black woman washing clothes in the river. Afterwards she got a part-time job at the airport. She drove a small vehicle in which she carried passengers from the Aviation Company. This job, which gave her a better income, made it possible for her to save and concentrate on her research.

One day when Moconga was walking through her district, a breeze blew and lifted her skirt. She quickly squeezed the fabric between her thighs. A passerby made a flirtatious remark to her and she continued on her way, unaffected. When she arrived at the restaurant, she became aware that she was listening to the same voice. Moconga felt that something made her happy inside. Someone greeted her from afar. She only caught the sound of the voice. The people who passed close to her were wearing casual clothes and walked slowly. Everything to control the heat.

Moconga intended to call a friend. She didn't want to be alone; she wanted to talk to someone. She thought that all human beings needed conversation, even those who thought they didn't need it. She felt that what she really wanted was a boyfriend. She became aware of little sparks; she longed for the company of a man, and she wanted to be caressed. She wanted a companion who appreciated what she was and she thought of a friend from university who was completing his doctoral thesis and always greeted her with a smile. His name was Henry Smart. Why hadn't it occurred to her she wondered¿ She went home with this thought although she supposed it could complicate her life. However, that evening she pondered how she could maintain a serious relationship with a man. Her eyes shone when she woke up. In her dreams, her hands had caressed the body of a man and his fingers touched her breasts. She could barely concentrate on her studies because, although she had not experienced love, she felt heartbeats, which made her smile. From then, she had faith in love and in her ability to have a meaningful relationship.

From that day, she went to work with more optimism and she was sprightly. Although she needed love, this feeling didn't torment her. It didn't become a fixed idea, which would drive her crazy. On the contrary, she allowed it to run its course naturally. She was accustomed to work and study and her savings grew. The idea of waiting didn't terrify her. Kimoto and Okio invited her regularly to their family reunions and were happy that Moconga had lost her initial fear.

Moconga found in her letterbox, an invitation to a lecture that Henry Smart was giving. The topic interested her and she attended but before leaving the house she prayed to Yemayá, the black goddess, whose role in her life was to give her security. She took a seat at the back in the last row of the auditorium. Before the event started, Henry went to greet her and to invite her sit in the front row. Moconga was embarrassed but instantly her security system against shyness began to function. Sports had helped her to develop her personality and with its magic power she had overcome the embarrassment of speaking in public. While she listened to the lecture she was formulating some questions in her mind. Smart was a young Negro from the Caribbean, with lively eyes and a broad smooth forehead. His mother was a lawyer, adviser to the President of Haiti. His father was an employee of the town council. Moconga thought of two questions and felt pleased with the replies. She was even encouraged to joke. Henry glanced at her in a meaningful way.

Afterwards those who attended went to a reception, an opportunity that Smart used to invite her to a movie. They went and when it was finished, they went to an ice cream shop. Moconga was surprised that he also was experiencing sadness because of not having someone with whom to converse. When the girl heard that familiar phrase, "I am attracted to you", she could no longer continue with that thread, which linked her to loneliness. Henry entered Moconga's heart. One Sunday she invited him to the home of Kimoto and Okio. They told her how much they wanted to see her holding hands with the young man. The married couple spoke with Henry and there was no news that gave them greater satisfaction than their engagement. They spoke about Moconga and from then every time the young couple visited them, they were received with pleasure.

Henry and Moconga were grateful for the encounter and were excited by every word that they heard. When the temperature improved and the sky became blue, they strolled through the gardens of the Japanese family in which azaleas bloomed. Nature in all her splendour seemed to celebrate the love affair of the couple. They would stop to look at the flowers and the squirrels; from time to time they shared secrets and laughed. Moconga informed her parents of the engagement to Henry Smart and months later they got married with the older Smarts attending. The neighbours saw the newly weds jogging at six in the afternoon, dressed in sneakers and caps.

Dr Moconga Smart was in Washington giving a seminar at the University of Melenda. She got off at the station to take the subway and was aware of how quickly night was falling. While she awaited the vehicle that would take her close to her house, she noticed a young black girl who was staring at her and moving her hands nervously. It was almost 7.00 p.m. and everybody was awaiting the subway anxiously so as to reach home soon. It seemed that the black woman was also waiting. She was wearing a very worn red jacket, black stockings and low-heeled shoes that had holes. She approached Moconga, told her that she had nowhere to spend the night and begged her to help. The woman's name was Luz Argentina Caicedo and she was in the country illegally. From that moment, Moconga thought of protecting the girl who had tearfully asked for help.

Moconga looked at her closely and smiled at her as if she had just agreed to her request. She felt pity for the young woman's state. Luz Argentina stood in silence, which seemed to indicate her gratitude as well as the fear of staying alone. She couldn't ask the lady's name and waited in anguish for the reply. When she tried to talk it was as if silence filled her mouth. She bit her lips. She felt a pressure at her temples and images appeared one on top of the other.

"Come with me."

As she arrived at the house, Luz Argentina began to cry. Her teeth chattered. After a cup of hot coffee, she recounted her arrival in the United States. Ruperto Cañarte forged a title of ownership so as to sell our red Ford in Izcaundé. Then we went to show it at the market. Men and women had gathered around an enormous number of vehicles. There were vehicles of all colours, sizes, brands and the owners explained to the clients the qualities and virtues of their vehicles. I stopped. The fear of not being able to get rid of our Ford was enormous. I went for my bag in which I had a bottle of cologne and put a little on my face to shake me out of my bewilderment. I polished the body of the car with a flannel cloth. Ruperto walked about from one side to the other until a young man came and asked the year of the car. Cañarte gave him the details but the client left. At midday a woman came who was interested in the details about the Ford. Ruperto convinced her of the good condition of the car and that she would be getting a bargain if she bought it from him. I was afraid she would discover that the vehicle was in poor condition but my husband came from a region where they knew how to sell, they were persons with business acumen. The lady bought the car. At times I believed that Ruperto could sell even bottled air. He acted with practical astuteness which eliminated anything superfluous in his offers. The lady paid in cash and Ruperto signed the receipt.

Through a fixer, Ruperto got two forged passports to travel to the United States. They cost three thousand dollars each and the negotiator had the responsibility of leaving us safe and sound in San Diego. The cost was paid with a portion of the money from the sale of the car. We arrived in Mexico and stayed in a house of modest appearance. There, a woman brought us a bowl of soup and a piece of bread. I did not eat. I was paralyzed with fear, huddled in the corner of the room. I stayed there without moving until a voice shook the atmosphere. It was time to depart. We got into a truck and hid ourselves among the sacks of potatoes. A group of persons who spoke softly travelled with us. We journeyed across the city until we came to a place where the driver told us to be silent and went to the road block to hand in the invoice for the cargo. At a crossroads, another truck awaited us. We changed vehicles rapidly and the first driver disappeared on the path.

Ruperto stayed beside me. All of us were nervous, alert and did not move. Suddenly three policemen stopped the vehicle. The driver showed his credentials and we resumed the journey. An hour later, a man who was hiding in the foliage appeared. We reversed and waited a long while in a clearing. A whistle sounded and the vehicle was allowed to go but we had not gone very far when it was stopped. Another patrolman asked the driver to come out of the truck. All of us held our breath and our bodies went cold. Blood rushed to my head and I got a headache. I looked at Ruperto. He was pale as if he were gravely ill, quiet, rigid as a corpse. We were paralysed by a great anxiety, by fear that the undertaking would fail. We had risked all the money we possessed and had even resorted to pawning the jewellery we had taken with us. Some of our travelling companions had sold their homes, signed IOUs and letters of commitment at high rates of interest. The anxiety decreased when we heard the order to depart. I touched Ruperto. His hand was cold. Suddenly I felt submerged in an underworld populated by unknown figures where I was surrounded by dead people. I remembered the death of the oldest person in the city, the death of the neighbour, the death of the porter at school. There were dead people and more dead people that I accumulated during my rambling until I came to the dead person I loved most, my Physics professor. Then I prayed that his spirit would protect us. I prayed to the souls in Purgatory to free us from all evil. I prayed that Immigration would not stop us and take us to the other side. I remained there thinking of the spirit of my teacher, concentrating, not even blinking, as if that spirit had become a part of me.

We arrived at dawn at Tijuana, the border between Mexico and the United States. We got out of the vehicle quickly and I could now see our travelling companions. They were of all ages, all colours, all professions, and all of us were dreaming of the seductive country. All of us saw it as marvellous and believed it was worth the sacrifice. We would get a job to recover the things we had pawned and then we would send money to our relatives and open a bank account.

We stopped in the shade of some huge trees and listened for the steps of the guard on the opposite bank of the River Sochate. Now it was a matter of waiting on the order to get into the water. It was necessary to synchronize movements, to be attentive to the signal and to swim until we reached San Diego. But the operation still didn't end there. A boat would pick us up to take us to a safe place.

At that hour the smell of chlorophyll floated like a delicate veil. We clung to the ground like ticks. We were in the most dangerous stretch of the crossing. Our faces were tired but we were pleased and considered ourselves heroes. Our character had hardened during the trip. We knew that we could perish at any moment but we were resolved to do everything. I believe that for Ruperto, crossing the border was the same as conquering a woman of exquisite beauty who with just one look ruled the universe. It was just like conquering the queen of the largest and richest kingdom in the world.

I started to tremble. I closed my eyes and was sure that I was dreaming. I refused to return to reality. I felt that I was dying or that I wanted to be dead. The icy wind cut through to my bones. I had a fever and the pain in my back made me uncomfortable when I breathed but I had to continue sniffing out danger. Afterwards nothing concerned me until I felt a push and when I opened my eyes I saw Ruperto running towards the river. I followed him quickly too. We had just a few minutes to reach the shore. Desperate, I lengthened my step and hurled myself into the river.

Moconga listened to her, intrigued. Luz Argentina took a breath. She was nervous and continued narrating her adventure. I moved my hands and feet like an insect with unsteady legs.

Since my parents got divorced I had longed to move away from solitude, to cut the umbilical cord that was growing and which tied me to the world of fatality. On land, Ruperto looked at me. We were soaked; we were 'wet backs'. I don't know if it was a look of protection or of pity.

While Moconga was bathing, Luz Argentina tidied the house and fixed breakfast. When she tasted it, Mrs. Smart intended to tell her that she should forget her life with Ruperto, that she should work and study. However, she thought that it was useless to speak to her about the matter. Why torment her anymore¿ It was better to let time pass. On her own she would adapt to her new situation. Luz Argentina looked at her with a blank expression and smiled coldly. Moconga was not brave enough to tell her the conditions under which she would receive her. She saw her as distant, afraid of the future with the fear that comes naturally from uncertainty.

The following week they left for Buffalo, where Henry was waiting for them. Luz Argentina was received affectionately. Up to that point she had only thought of earning a living by working, even if it were cleaning floors. The next day the couple took her to learn the route to get to the subway station.

Moconga took on the task of getting her a job in a Latin restaurant. There, she would wash plates and clean up the kitchen.

The work was so hard that Caicedo would get home tired to the point where she had no desire to study but after resting an hour, she felt a sudden enthusiasm to dance to African rhythms. She sang *caderonas* and in this way recovered her energy. In this way she regained the desire to study the new language. When she started to think in English, the words and the streets had a different meaning for her. She then sought a better paying job. She wrote to her mother so that she would send her documents to her, which were in the archives of the university.

She got a job in a factory. Now she put children's clothes on hangers but those objects were so difficult to open that they hurt her fingers. She was not permitted to speak and Luz Argentina took advantage of the silence to mentally revise her English classes. The following month they transferred her to another section where she stuffed babies' shoes with paper. The work seemed simple but she had to bend down to pick up the paper, then straighten up, fix the item and place it on the shelf above her head. The speed with which she had to do the work didn't allow her even a few minutes of rest. After two months she felt pain in her spine but as she was there illegally she had no social welfare. The cheques she received did not go very far as they deducted 30 per cent for the company that got her the job, 20 per cent went for transport and 30 per cent for the lunch served in the factory.

Moconga got her a job in a family home. The advantage of having free accommodation, food and other benefits suited her. There, she looked after a sick woman, and helped with the cooking and tidying of the house. This job allowed her to save and to send to her mother what she needed. After Luz Argentina stayed a year in this home, Moconga and a lawyer legalized her status in the country.

For Luz Argentina, the plan to study at university became an obsession, latent in everything she achieved. She did everything well so that her employers would not fire her. This goal was her consolation. She had promised herself to forget Ruperto who disappeared without telling her why. Perhaps he died in one of his usual quarrels with Latinos or the Immigration caught him and locked him up or perhaps he found another woman who was more profitable for him.

Luz Argentina Caecido asked no questions of anyone nor did she inform the police for fear of being deported or imprisoned. She waited for him until her meagre savings were exhausted then she put on her jacket and set out in search of work. It was then that she met Moconga, a black woman like her. She recognized her mistakes in betraying Susana Garcés but, at that time, she thought it was a youthful thing to play with destiny. She wasn't capable of imagining anything more amusing and exciting. She understood it in this way; then it seemed to her that the idea of running away with Ruperto had a particular meaning and was a question of intelligence. She believed that her destiny was linked to Cañarte's. He displayed wisdom and great experience. Afterwards she understood that her betrayal of her friend was not just a minor matter as if it were a colleague, a neighbour or a client. It was an act that possibly traumatized Susana Garcés for her whole life and made her distrustful of everyone from that moment onwards. She wouldn't be surprised if someone would betray her also, and the worst thing was that the deceptions could have left a lasting impression on Susana's memory and deformed her soul.

After Luz Argentina's betrayal of her childhood playmate, she couldn't be the same. She would have lost faith in human beings and she supposed that her friend would never forget her terrible experience. She was not a fortune-teller, nor did she wish any future evil on Susana, but after so much time, Luz Argentina thought that her mistake had damaged both of them.

One winter morning, Luz Argentina Caicedo with amazement and sadness remembered Susana Garcés. During her first months in the United States, she felt disturbed within herself at what had happened and believed she was released from her action. Susana was not, still, married to Ruperto so it was not a significant fact, but as time passed she began to feel that she was walking in a desert and even worse that she was a desert, and began to assess the facts.

At times she didn't understand why she fled with Ruperto, why she was crazy about him as he was no more than a nonentity escaped from hell. As if to taunt her, Cañarte began to remember Susana, continually praised her virtues and celebrated those moments when he had been with her. He complained about his fate having left Susana Garcés. It wasn't his fault but Luz Argentina's because to achieve her plans he used the mask of lies. When unexpectedly he praised Luz Argentina, his compliment was insincere, a mockery, a satire.

When he spoke to Luz Argentina Caicedo, he wanted to make it clear that because of her intelligence he had lost Susana. Luz Argentina noticed how being intelligent became something negative, a fault. "You are bright, very intelligent," he said looking mockingly at her.

Luz Argentina Caicedo bowed her head and deduced that her intelligence could lead her as much to betrayal as to acquiring a profession. Horrified, she looked at Ruperto while he continued smiling. Every day when they both returned from work, he debased her talent. Then she cursed her flight with that man. She would never forgive herself for her sin. Luz Argentina didn't like to remember what she had done. Destiny had made them unfortunate and she was especially sad because Susana Garcés was of her race, black like her. Both had suffered the same discriminations; both were poor; both had the same desires. But she realized that at that time she committed crazy acts without considering the consequences. Her aspiration was to leave that town. When the first conflicts with Ruperto took place, she was afraid and at night cried silently when she understood that they were separated by an abyss that grew deeper each day and that it did not allow them to have even a basic relationship. Luz Argentina didn't know how to remedy the situation; she felt weak: he had destroyed her self-esteem.

That day she walked in search of a new job but once they saw her they told her that there was no vacancy. She began to feel engulfed in solitude and uncertainty and hunger tormented her. Her shoes, full of holes and patched with cardboard, were soaking wet. She cried; she needed her mother. She walked, balancing herself; she shouldn't allow herself to be overwhelmed by failure and remorse. She would create a fantasy world in which there was no place for pessimism or poverty. She would find work she told herself; her mother's soul would protect her and she clung to the idea that she would find something. She went towards the subway and there she found Moconga when night was falling on the Washington skyscrapers.

Three months after Moconga gave birth, Luz Argentina left for Washington to study at the University of Melenda, which had awarded her a scholarship to pursue studies in Literature. Moconga embraced her friend with happy tenderness while Luz Argentina felt the antithesis between solidarity and betrayal. Moconga had made her understand that the human being can give love. The two friends looked at each other face to face. It was a look of absolute confidence for success. That absolute confidence that Moconga had in her friend made Luz Argentina bow her head because she remembered her disloyalty. She walked towards the crib where Toney, Moconga and Henry's son, was sleeping. She took him in her arms and said some words of love to him, wishing for him that Changó would protect him throughout his life.

Henry took Luz Argentina's suitcase and put it in the car and they left for the airport. For her, time had become magical and she invented at that moment, a word which meant gratitude, generosity or something more: *yampa*. This was what the human being lost when God expelled him from Paradise, converting him into a being opposite to what he had been. At the instance of his expulsion, the human being became narcissistic and forgot *yampa*. Luz Argentina recovered the word gratitude that in the past had been erased from her vocabulary. They embraced.

During the flight to Washington, Luz Argentina could not avoid thinking of Susana and across the distance she imagined her smile. Her mother had written to her telling her that she had a baby named Isis; that the baby was white skinned with black eyes, a flat nose and curly hair; that they drove her to her Grandma Carlota's house. Luz Argentina was aware that she was on the road to success. She wouldn't take one step backwards as there was no possibility of return. The events of life don't return and life is not written as a rough copy. Life taught her not to play tricks. She believed when she was an adolescent that she could spend time having fun without suffering remorse, but now it was different. The crux of the matter was in understanding that she had only one path, one goal that she would achieve. She remembered the sad night when Hernán Cortés arrived to conquer Mexico. He ordered all the ships to be burned, removing all possibility of return, so he and his soldiers risked everything. His motto was victory or death.

Four years later, Luz Argentina travelled to Atlanta to present a paper on Afro-Hispanic myths. At that time she taught Spanish language at the university, as her scholarship stipulated. On Friday afternoons she would use the common room to give classes. Everyday she ate at home as she did not want to forget the food of her country and sometimes invited one or two friends to taste what she had prepared.

When she arrived at the university auditorium in Atlanta, the editor of Channel 32 Television was awaiting her. He interviewed her and she demonstrated, while laughing and joking, how to dance *la caderona*. The announcer, Stanley Richards, a black man, two meters in height, praised her skill in transmitting the tropical emotion.

Luz Argentina began her presentation by saying that the first African tribe, the first in the world, was called the Mursi,the embryo of humanity. Africa has a long history of navigation and a rich archaeology which clearly proved its presence in America before the arrival of Columbus. After two days, Luz Argentina received a telephone call from Stanley Richards who spoke to her of love at first sight and of the chemistry of feelings. He said he did not like to hide his emotions when it came to the opposite sex. Luz Argentina's heart began to beat with new strength; she began to feel pleasantly excited. She felt the anguish of being and not being. She saw the sea full of trees and trains. She forgot death.

Everything continued in apparent calm. Marvin reconciled once again the two women he loved. The unfortunate days remained in the past. He recommended not stoking the fires as the flames could burn up everybody. One year later, his prediction became a reality.

Margarita became tolerant, a change that neutralized her contempt for me. Jaime seemed indifferent to his father's conflicts and walked as if he were in the air, always involved with his girlfriends who telephoned him at all hours. When the phone rang at dawn it was one of his lovers telling him that she was waiting for him. One night he communicated to Marvin his wish to play the *guitarra*. I refused to give him classes, as his contempt for me was strong. All of us in the home turned to Divine Providence. We were afraid and feared another scandal. Besides, no one wanted to be the loser. Margarita walked with her head bowed and stayed in her room watching television. Jaime would arrive at dawn, filling the atmosphere with his breath heavy with alcohol, his hair dishevelled and with the scorching smell of feminine perfumes. He never said a word but his body odours poured out, which was his way of speaking, of reiterating to the world where his passion lay. He went through the house, moving along the corridors, listening to music at the highest pitch. He would phone his girlfriends, put on weekend parties and from time to time was given to bursts of youthfulness. He walked as if he were flying. He was like a feather floating in the air. In contrast, his sister seated in Ruth's rocking chair, was like a statue, and like a statue, completely inoffensive.

When I came out of class I would see Marvin in the car. He was desperate to arrive on time. We would go to the port to eat his favourite dish, grilled lobster with slices of fried plantain. On one occasion we met Carlos Zambrano. We greeted each other politely. He, for reasons connected to work, had changed university so he was no longer my colleague. That night a trio was singing songs by Los Panchos. I asked them to accompany me and we sang "La Momposina", which was a premonition because when we arrived home Luz Argentina appeared accompanied by Stanley Richards. He was dressed in a dashiki with African figures and spoke Spanish. Luz Argentina stretched out her arms to me and we remained embraced for a long while. She laughed and we held hands like when we were children. Marvin kissed her on her cheek and jumped for joy. All of us laughed because of the happy meeting. We opened a bottle of whiskey and said "cheers", clinking the glasses. We went to the kitchen and prepared fish using Ruperto's recipe. While we made the sauce, we laughed and without saying it, refused to add more misfortunes to our lives. Luz Argentina still wore clothing made of lycra, had her hair in braids and wore earrings, while I had a new image. Laughter seemed to revitalize her and her large black eyes seemed even brighter. There was no time to talk of good and evil, we were just happy. In that state of liveliness, Jaime joined the party and in the blink of an eye we began to dance while Isis was sleeping at her grandparents' house. Marvin made an effort to follow my rhythm and to forget his tango steps, which he used for all types of music. Luz Argentina and Stanley glided along slowly. Jaime stopped in front of me and we danced a *bolero*. His arms circled my waist; his cheek rubbed mine; I breathed his racehorse odour. He glanced at me and squeezed his hands tighter. I had never felt him so close; I had never experienced anything like this. My breath was short and my heart beat faster. We remembered when we were children and we bathed naked in the rain. The music stopped and we sat in a corner of the room and he just looked at me. I noticed his piercing eyes and saw him dry his lips with his hand. Tiredness overcame us. Stanley and Luz Argentina went to a seaside resort to continue their honeymoon.

In bed, I made an effort to control my secret fear of Margarita. Sometimes Marvin's word came to me – Leave! Before that, he was my idol, my reason for living, but that idolatry was a thing of the past. I was insecure at his side, believing myself happy and enjoying the peace that I had created. We had both become dream weavers. Margarita remained watchful, her anger increasing daily, masked in heavy silences. At nights she spent a long time watching the clear sky; at times a tear fell from her blue eyes. Now it was a battle to the death with me. I thought that a new plan must be developing in her brain against me and my little daughter. For this reason, Isis spent the day with Carlota and Joelí.

She went to early mass, offered her prayers for the soul of her mother. For a while she looked at the Christ raised above the main altar as if it were the first time she was seeing it and she told him her plan. She, as the oldest daughter of the family, had the responsibility of removing the dishonour, of removing the bandage from her father's eyes. She put her hand on her breast, heard the beating of her heart and begged God pardon in case she was mistaken.

Perhaps some remote being could justify my father but not I. He is imbued with the idea of the rights that Negroes have, that we are all equal, that they are rational beings and that they have worthy feelings. For this reason, he married a black woman. That woman does not love him. Just by looking at her face it is obvious that the only things that interest her are the money and social position of my father. It's very comfortable to think that he is right while his friends laugh at him behind his back. When she reached the house, she went up to her stepmother.

"I'm giving this to you as a gift; it was my mother's bracelet."

I smiled when I received it. I realized that the time had come for me to be more careful for myself and to fear for Isis' life. The gift symbolized a warning of danger. The months passed and I did not fully understand the reason for Margarita's change. I imagined that she had accepted second place as the running of the house was now in my power.

"She has given up," I told myself.

On Friday nights on the terrace, Marvin listened to me playing the *guitarra* and singing. His ears alert, he leaned forward so as to hear better. Jaime would arrive early and he accompanied us. Marvin put my *guitarra* in his son's hands for me to teach him to play. I went close to him to show him how to place his fingers on the strings. When my face was close to him he made flirtatious gestures. The apprenticeship was slow and I encountered the problem that my student had no musical talent, or he was unable to overcome his resentment toward me. But when Jaime learned to strum, Marvin felt happy. His son was a worthy descendant of Mary Clark who was a skilful piano player. One evening we heard laughter from Luz Argentina and Stanley who came to say goodbye.

She brought the photos of us dressed as artists. This time, we both laughed. Now there was no distance between us. We sought reasons to bring up memories and we ended up mentioning Ruperto.

"That devil went off and left me alone," said Luz Argentina laughing loudly.

We said goodbye with an embrace that seemed to us unending.

"Come and visit us," said Luz Argentina as she gave me her card.

Margarita would seek an opportunity to amuse herself with her father and me when we returned home after spending the afternoon with Isis. She seemed to have accepted her defeat and it wasn't the first time that she came to me as if to show that all resentment had ended. I was unable to understand that attitude and kept my unease latent but I breathed a little calmly on thinking that my stepdaughter's hate had come to an end, that that perpetual insane feeling had ended. But, at times, I also believed that her resignation was a bad omen.

So, in a spontaneous way, when there were no classes at the university and our daughter was sleeping at my mother's house, Margarita suggested to us that we play the card game 'Forty'. She and Jaime were partners, as were Marvin and I. We served several glasses of whiskey with coca cola and slices of lemon. I didn't think that my stepdaughter's astuteness could be so refined. She did nothing that would make me suspect a trap. She lived in two worlds: one as a bank official where she performed efficiently and honourably and another in which her love for her dead mother had only one objective: vengeance.

From then on, Sunday after Sunday, we settled down to play. The card games, the laughter, the jokes, the whiskey eased the tension. We achieved an atmosphere of happiness and afterwards we felt a sort of need to get together this way. We all benefited from exchanging affection and little by little we got rid of the burden of hate and resentment. I thought that was healthy for my daughter. Margarita, proving her skill in planning entertainment, alternated the activities. Sometimes we went to the country and took our daughter and played with her.

Margarita limited herself to giving her a balloon. She said she liked animals more than children. Jaime smiled at Isis. Then Marvin remembered the picnics with his parents and brother. We roasted chicken or mullets for lunch. We sat in the shade and Jaime reviewed his guitar classes or went to the club and after Marvin and his son jogged they went to the sauna. Margarita went to the gym and I stayed with Isis. On other occasions I took my civil law book and studied under an acacia tree while they slept. We had completely forgotten Ruth and we chatted while listening to the trill of the birds and watching their flight.

One Sunday we returned home early as rain forced us to leave the resort and Marvin started to cough and run a fever. Margarita brought home a canary that she found on the way with its wings broken. Jaime went to the market for a cage. She gave it bread soaked in milk and called a veterinarian to cure it.

That month we didn't go out. Marvin had caught a cold. His discomfort had scarcely begun when he begged us not to let him die. I put compresses of limewater on his forehead and gave him coca cola boiled with brown sugar. It was the first time that I saw him ill. I was shocked at the intensity of his horror of death, at journeying through other worlds. Isis was enjoying her grandparents' world. It was the time when Jaime and I took the opportunity to practise the *guitarra* on the terrace in the nights and to chat extensively. He spoke to me of his marvellous world and cautiously awakened my dormant desires, especially when we read the novel *Lady Chatterley's Lover*. Marvin complained about how his son spent money. He took his girlfriends to eat in luxurious restaurants and showered them with several gifts. The university woods and the faculty bathrooms were his preferred places, not so much for himself but because his girlfriends experienced urgent desires. Marvin found it strange that he studied so assiduously on the terrace. His son had become a homebody.

Jaime sang with me on moonlight nights as the lessons

progressed. On one occasion Margarita brought her transistor radio and with some drinks of rum, we livened up the hours. The closeness with my stepchildren gave me more security and soon the class, with the music from the radio, became a dance. He taught me the latest *merengue* and *salsa* steps. He opened his arms and held my hands so that I could learn the turns.

Margarita was seated in a corner on the terrace and hate boiled in her and flowered with the strength of an orgasm, an evil joy, which forced her to smile when she saw her stepmother dancing in the arms of her brother. Susana laughed, her full mouth enlarged by the tattoo around her lips, her eyes shone with liner, her Sophia Loren eyebrows and her straightened hair, which hung to her shoulders. How different she was now! It took a lot of effort not to throw her down on the terrace. Perhaps she thought of Isis.

Marvin recovered and went early in the morning to an acupuncturist to have needles inserted in the meridians of his body. I went to mass and a great confusion overwhelmed me to the point that I could not organize my thoughts. My conscience was confused and I needed to be close to God. In church I cried because in bed I felt Jaime's breath. He was the magician of the labyrinths. He knew the magic to excite his labyrinths and mine. After listening to the words of the priest, I went home and had a cold shower. I took infusions of lemon balm for my nerves. I spent seven days fasting to get away from thinking of Jaime and his erotic movements. Nevertheless, a sweet temptation entered the cracks of the bedroom, an energizing temptation that intoxicated me and made me float like a leaf in the wind. I fell on my knees begging. The voice of my stepson resonated in my depths. Then I noticed the smell of the rat and, at times, her scratching on the door even seemed pleasant to me.

I felt a desire to belong to the church choir and Marvin welcomed the idea as it brought back to him memories of his mother. Just the idea of listening to religious songs increased his love and admiration for me. I sang sweetly to the Virgin to save me from torture. The card games started again and Margarita chose me to be her partner. Again the liquor, jokes, smiles and laughter. The drinks flushed Jaime's face with joy. His eyes were two high tides that attracted me like magnets with a power I could not resist. I imagined holding Jaime's hand as we entered the labyrinths we made on the beach when we were children. A telephone call interrupted the game. Marvin left hurriedly. A fire near to the bank forced him to stay in his office until he saw that the calamity had ended.

The following Sunday we settled down to play cards through the night. The slow rhythm of a *cumbia* was heard while the cards sounded on the table. Jaime put a card on his forehead and the sweat made it stick. Marvin tried to guess which card it could be. Suddenly I felt warm fingers sliding on my thigh. It was Jaime's hand passing me an eight of diamonds for a win. We passed many cards like this, he touching my thigh, I caressing his legs. Afterwards passing cards didn't matter to us, just the delicious contact. A kind of asphixia caused me to breathe deeply while silently I was saying, "Oh God, this can't be, give me strength." I couldn't accept it. I should move back the chair but his fingers made me tremble with pleasure. I was living in a world of panic and fantasies. Those fingers set my arteries on fire. I had never imagined such delight. Jaime looked at me piercingly, his laugh full of alcohol and each time he became more daring. He brought his chair a little closer so that his knees found mine. I knew him well. He appeared unperturbed. I was afraid. I tried to move my legs but he imposed his will and prevented me with his foot. Now, another of Margarita's jokes and, as I laughed, two tears escaped. I murmured something unintelligible. We were playing by candlelight and everything that was happening was dangerous and incredibly marvellous.

"Forty," Marvin said and threw his cards on the table.

I believed I was accustomed to strong emotions but I felt a

wave of conflicting emotions, a sudden fear that gave me a cold sweat. In bed, I imagined Jaime's hands groping for me. The need to tell Marvin what was happening tortured me but I remembered what he told me before our honeymoon ended: "I forbid you to say even one word, which could make me bitter towards my children." I closed my eyes and saw my body on the chest of drawers as my grandmother, Matilde, advised me. I touched the nipples of my breasts. My curves had not deteriorated even slightly. How difficult it was to stop that torrent of energy! Mama's rooster woke us up singing. I heard it in the distance. It was impossible to tell Marvin, it would be better to let time run its course.

Marvin was away from the city because of the opening of a branch of the bank and I went to my parents' house, fleeing from my confused desires. I bathed Isis, dressed her in the prettiest dress she had, braided her hair and decorated it with red ribbons and then I sat down to study. I studied the lessons in a loud voice to get Jaime out of my mind but inside me something unusual was throbbing. Bent over Isis' crib, my eyes filled with tears. I was in distress, I wasn't sure of myself.

Mama noticed my nervousness and mentioned it when she smelled my blouse before washing it.

"Are you having a problem, daughter¿"

I denied such a thing. When he returned, Marvin passed by the house. He embraced Isis, for whom he had brought a sleeping doll. Mama suggested to him that he should take care of me as I wasn't well. Marvin put his arms around my waist and squeezed me.

"Is something wrong, my darling¿"

"No, no, why¿"

Jaime disguised his anguished desires and walked from one side to another. Sometimes I saw him sitting with his eyes closed, perhaps to engrave my image more deeply in his mind. We looked at each other closely and communicated silently like accomplices. I walked on tiptoe, gliding like a shadow and this increased the desires of my stepson.

Margarita invited us to the swimming pool at a private resort for the weekend. I refused to go on the pretext of an exam on the Tuesday but Marvin insisted. Always indulgent to his daughter, he suggested that I should take advantage of the rest, given my state of health as my mother had told him to take care of me. Isis stayed in mama's care.

Little by little the sun was getting warm. Marvin stretched out his towel on the solarium. He put coconut oil on his face and covered it with the newspaper. Margarita met a friend and they disappeared. I saw them going off arm in arm. Jaime and I tanned in the sun and this increased our torment. Submerged in the water we enjoyed rubbing together. When he rubbed against my breast, I felt in Jaime the delicious taste of forbidden fruit. He, under the water, caressed my waist; I, the hairs on his chest, with a pleasure each time more intense. I could not find strength to stop him from kissing my lips. I had no will power to protect myself from those forces. We were the same age. We had the same heat of youth, the same emotions, identical pleasures. Moreover, I believed that his desires would be accompanied by resentment and revenge because he had the intensity of passion.

Suddenly Marvin, standing at the edge of the swimming pool, saw us. His jealousy spread through his entire body, his face was red and his eyes danced about. He refused to eat. Perhaps he wondered if we were capable of betrayal. On the contrary, I was living the sincerity of the lie. It seemed impossible for me to take a step backwards. Something was dragging me desperately into Jaime's arms. It was a way of experiencing life without regrets, the consuming, invincible force of instinct.

Marvin left the city for several days on secondment, perhaps to test my attitude or to show he was not jealous, or because of dignity, or that something that we have within when danger calls us, with the premonition of being on the point of losing everything. He left me at my parents. Now when Marvin spoke to me his voice sounded like the emptiness of a catacomb. He realized that he was no longer receiving my tenderness in our relations. He followed my steps so as to get me far away from Jaime. He was living in a storm. He was not sure of me anymore and kept going around the house changing from distrust to dejection. He suggested to me that we move from the house, that we live outside the city in a small, more cozy villa. His children were young; they could conquer life; they wouldn't need him.

"Darling, I am old now."

After what occurred at the swimming pool, he realized that he had aged, as if time was weighing on him more heavily than before.

He entered a world of shadows. He no longer read love poems. When he came home from the office he went to Ruth's rocking chair and stayed there like a man condemned to death. I spent a great deal of time at my parents' house and with Isis. I rarely saw Jaime. Sometimes we met in the dining room and then it seemed to me that he was an unbridled horse and I, a mare in heat. Marvin invited his son to share his leisure hours for one reason or another, perhaps desirous of copying Jaime's youth.

He insisted on leaving that house where Ruth had lived but I did not accept the suggestion. How to get away from that magnetic flow? How to separate myself from that angel or devil that was my fascination?

"This house is big; it has Persian carpets, oil paintings, lamps, tapestries, mirrors. We live close to my parents. They look after Isis."

Surely he remembered the words that he had said to me years before? We went on a trip to Brazil to the carnival in Rio de Janeiro. He understood that the best thing would be to leave the house for a while, that another honeymoon would be good for him.

He subjected himself to a feverish rhythm in the gym. He went to the homeopath to strengthen those parts of him that were failing and when the treatment with KH3 was finished, we left on vacation.

While we looked at fifty thousand samba dancers go by, divided into fifteen groups, showing the beauty of body and rhythm, I felt the need for another type of love. For me, Jaime with his crazy acts filled me. He measured time in another dimension; he didn't walk on the earth; he was a dazzling condor. That way, lazy, breaking with routine, improvising, enjoying the disorder, moving about from here to there without fear, irreverent, that way I loved him. He faced life flippantly while his father was tied to order and formality. Those Brazilian dancers, with their bottoms exposed and their attractive tempting figures, created in me the idea to search for a love that would leave me satisfied. When the parade ended, I was a woman more desirous of Jaime. Marvin gazed into my eyes, worried. I could do nothing now. There was no remedy. I went in search of a *guitarra* and while I sang for him, my thoughts were flying to irresistible desires. My memory went to the days when I played with Jaime in the rain, hair dishevelled, he soaping my back and laughing his crazy laughter. Marvin understood that my songs were not for him, that someone was between us.

We both tried to hide reality, determined to conceal our thoughts. I didn't enjoy his caresses now without thinking of the pleasure of being in the arms of his son. He had made me into a different person. I couldn't enjoy Marvin fully. I was a zombie. I thought only of Jaime and believed that it was with him that I was making love.

Indifferent, we visited the tourist spots of Rio de Janeiro. We set out on tours acting like mad persons, but at times we looked at each other with a certain resentment. We went up in the cable car to Sugar Loaf Mountain; I looked at the landscape from those heights and realized that jealousy was beginning to gnaw at his thoughts and that he was now feeling like a back row spectator. We continued the trip without feelings of guilt. We toured the city and controlled the situation by admiring the beauty of Rio de Janeiro.

On returning home, Marvin was very indulgent towards his son. They chatted animatedly and Marvin suggested sending him to Grandmother Mary, to the United States. Jaime smiled, looking at me entranced as a believer looks at sacred images. I ran to mama's house and took refuge in the arms of Isis.

One Friday night Marvin got an urgent call. They had tried to hold up the bank. He took his revolver; I told him to be careful; he kissed me and left. Sitting on the bed, I thought of the possibility that Ruperto had returned. While I was awaiting news, I heard the handle of the bedroom door turn slowly. I saw a silhouette. I could not identify the person who was entering. He walked softly on the carpet. Then I made out the familiar cat eyes. I was afraid; the rhythm of my blood changed. I heard Jaime's agitated breathing. The long-awaited moment of triumph had come but fear became silent, which seemed to indicate acceptance or perhaps fear of feeling his colt's breath. How¿ Why reject him if I had been preparing myself for the moment¿ His gaze rested on my lips; I felt the touch of his fingers on my breasts. The spell of love had come. The moon inspired our oblivion.

Marvin found her in the bedroom with her legs exposed, revealing parts of her genitals. The noise of the rat, which was scratching the wall, woke her. Then she saw Marvin aiming his revolver at them.

"Guardian Angel, protect me," murmured Susana.

"Father!" exclaimed Jaime and hastily began to cover himself. Marvin hesitated, undecided as to whom to kill. She smiled, perhaps believing she would be pardoned, perhaps to get God's pity or perhaps to maintain her smile after death. Marvin remained rigid, determined to administer justice. He weighed the gravity of blame so as not to err in the punishment.

His suspicions had been confirmed and he asked himself, "What should I do now¿"

Perhaps return to solitude, perhaps die because of dishonour and sadness, perhaps commit suicide or perhaps kill them. Confused, he could not think. He could decide nothing, nothing that could separate him from Susana.

•••

Translators'Notes

"Sochate" (p.134): This is the word as it appears in the original Spanish. The author clearly creates a context where persons are crossing from Mexico into the USA via a river ("Sochate"). There is a river, the Suchiate, which separates Guatemala from Mexico and is frequently used by Hispanics in South and Central America to gain access into Mexico and from there to the USA. *Editor's comment*: 'Suchiate' has its linguistic origin in the Nahuatl word 'Xochiate' (meaning 'flower water'). The two seem to be combined in Caicedo's narrative and in the author's depiction of her dramatic reemergence – the denouement of another very distinct and important strand, Luz Argentina Caicedo's story. She tells us that they "arrived at dawn at Tijuana... and listened for the steps of the guard on the opposite bank of the River Sochate" (p.134). Let's look at what Lori Saldaña, a journalist writing in the June 1994 San Diego *Earth Times* (http://www.sdearthtimes. com/et0694/et0694s1.html), tells us about theTijuana River Valley, and determine if Chiriboga intentionally fictionalizes and plays on place names, etc. in some of Caicedo's accounts in order to help us appreciate more fully the depth of turmoil and confusion of her troubled mind, particularly in the wake of the gruelling experiences at the border, Cañarte's disappearance and her obviously unstable condition, and trapped as she is in the haunting memories of her betrayal of Susana:

> The valley lies immediately north of the U.S.-Mexico border, between San Ysidro and Interstate 5 to the east, the Pacific Ocean to the west.... The river running through this broad, green landscape receives its water from creeks, streams and other small tributaries draining some 1,700 square miles.... The river *crosses the international border* east of Interstate 5 and meanders northwest for about five miles before reaching the ocean.... The river winds its way through lots owned by private parties, the city and county of San Diego.... (emphasis the editor's)

References to the University of 'Melenda' (p.139) where she studied; and to the 'Mursi' ('Morrys' in the original *En la noche*) as the "first African tribe, the first in the world... the embryo of humanity" (p.141) may also be part of the same fabric. In this latter case, the translators call our attention to the very primitive Ethiopian tribe, the Mursi, and advise that it replace 'Morrys' but caution that there is no evidence to show the Mursi to be "the first".